The Winter of Enchantment

THE WINTER
OF
ENCHANTMENT

VICTORIA WALKER

THE BOBBS-MERRILL COMPANY, INC.

Indianapolis   New York

THE BOBBS-MERRILL COMPANY, INC.
A SUBSIDIARY OF HOWARD W. SAMS & CO., INC.
PUBLISHERS INDIANAPOLIS KANSAS CITY NEW YORK

CONTENTS

From his perch on the window seat Sebastian watched the November gusts scatter the heaps of leaves, toss each one in the air and then blow them into new piles. The trees looked awkward, their branches spiky and black. They peered sadly at their reflections cast on the gutter water, which choked and dribbled through the dams made by the street litter and leaves.

It was afternoon, and the sky was grey and heavy. It looked as if it were being held up by the pointed roofs of the London houses. The horses and carriages rocked and rattled past the window where Sebastian sat, and the familiar sound was comforting. It made the mournful trees and the hanging sky seem majestic instead of gloomy. The library fire was burning bright and orange, and was the only light in the room, so that vast shadows stood in corners and lurked among the shelves. Sebastian was not in the least nervous, though. He always felt that the shadows had as much right to use the library as he did and would in fact have been lonely if he had had to spend these dark winter afternoons without them.

It would soon be time for tea and Mrs Parkin would come bustling in to light the lamps, and the shadows would slip quickly through the walls and under the floors to find another quiet place to stand and brood. Sebastian rested his forehead against the cold glass and watched the windows

7

grow from grey to yellow in the houses opposite, as the families gathered together for their tea. He wondered if his father would be having his tea alone, and then he remembered that time in India is not the same as it is in England, and it would not be tea-time there but probably dinner-time or even the middle of the night.

He thought about the letter he'd had that morning from his father. It had said that he would be coming home in a month's time, bringing his new wife with him. Also that he had a surprise for him, which he thought would make him very happy, but Sebastian would have to wait until his return to find out what it was.

Sebastian's mother had died when he was three. That was ten years ago, and since then he and his father had managed very well with Mrs Parkin and her niece, Sarah, to look after them. William looked after the carriage and horses, and Sylvester looked after his father's business affairs. Sebastian could not remember his mother at all, he had only a large portrait on the stairs to tell him what she had been like. She was dressed all in white, and sitting in a garden among trees and long grasses, so the effect of the painting was all white and green except for the little bird on her hand, which was pale turquoise.

Sebastian was shaken out of the dreaming doze he had fallen into by the clatter of the tea-tray, Mrs Parkin's solid tread on the stair, and the click of the library door opening.

'Sitting in the dark, again, you funny child?' said Mrs Parkin. As she stood in the doorway, the bun on her head looked exactly like an orange balanced on the top of a big curvy shape. She put the tray down and lit the gas lamps. The shadows wavered and melted away. Her round shining face appeared out of the gloom and Sebastian smiled at her with affection. The silver teapot glistened and steamed. The pile of toast wobbled uncertainly, and then slid into a heap.

8

'How was Latin this morning?' she said, as she arranged the tea things.

'Oh, all right, I suppose. I don't think I'll ever be very good at it,' said Sebastian, sadly.

'Well I've never done a word of it myself, and I've managed so I dare say you will too.' Mrs Parkin was a very cheering person to be with, she always made life seem easier than you thought it was. 'Have you finished your homework, Sebastian? The others will be going out this evening so I thought we could have a nice cosy supper in the kitchen together.'

'Lovely. Yes, I have done it. There wasn't much today.'

'Rightio then, have your tea and then pop out for a walk or something, and I'll have it ready by half-past six.'

A moment later and she was plodding down the stairs again. Sebastian was hungry and quickly finished his tea. Then he sat back and gazed at the teapot, wondering if he should go for a walk. The teapot had been brought back by his father from one of his many journeys abroad. In certain lights and from a certain angle you could see a man's face on it, with a beard and heavy eyebrows, and very wrinkled. Sebastian looked at the strange face. Then he jumped. Surely he was mistaken? Just for a moment he thought that he had seen the teapot wink at him! He looked harder. It wasn't usual for teapots to wink at people, he reminded himself, it was probably just the flickering of the firelight. The face grinned back at him and, just as Sebastian was beginning to feel silly about staring out a teapot, it slowly and deliberately dropped its silver eyelid and raised it again. Sebastian rubbed his eyes. He was probably more imaginative than a good many children, but nothing like this had ever happened to him before. When he picked up the teapot and looked at it closely, it was just as it had always been, and he could run his fingers over the face and find it quite solid. He decided

9

that he would go for a walk which always helped him to think, so he went downstairs to find his coat and boots.

Pulling his tartan muffler tighter round his throat, he stepped out into the street. The gusts were stronger now, and everyone was hurrying to get home. They didn't notice the small boy with untidy brown hair and grey eyes standing on the pavement, watching the traffic rush by. The breath of the horses as they snorted and strained made great coils of mist, and the black, lumbering shapes of the hansom cabs seemed to miss each other only by inches as they leaned from side to side, springs groaning and squeaking.

Sebastian started to walk along the street, and after a

time he no longer noticed what was going on around him. He was thinking about the teapot and what it could possibly mean, for he was certain now that he had not imagined it. After half an hour's walking he was still quite baffled and beginning to feel cold. When he looked around to find the quickest way back, he found that he'd walked much further than he'd intended. Fortunately he remembered that he'd been this way before and he knew that by following the back streets he would easily be home in time for supper. It was almost fully dark now and growing colder all the time, and just as Sebastian turned the corner into a narrow little street, a few snowflakes fell before him. Soon they were going down his neck, gathering on his eyelashes, making the toes of his black boots wet and shiny and falling thicker and faster every minute. It was useless to try and hurry, the pavements were slippery and he kept banging into everyone else. So he walked quite slowly, glancing up now and then to watch the flakes hurtling down from the dark sky. Then a commotion was caused by a carriage which was trying to take a short cut down the narrow street. All the passers-by had to crowd back against the fronts of the buildings to avoid being sprayed from head to foot with slush. Sebastian made for a shop doorway nearby, and found himself almost trampled underfoot by the hoard of people who had chosen the same doorway to hide from the flying mud and snow. In fact there was so much shoving and pushing that the door behind Sebastian gave way with a gentle click and he found himself separated from the crowd and the weather, and standing in what appeared to be a dark and rather gloomy furniture shop.

An old man and a young man were standing in one corner, talking to each other, and they didn't seem to have noticed Sebastian's arrival. They continued to talk as if he wasn't there. He was afraid of letting in an avalanche of people if he opened the door again, so he decided to wait for a few moments, and, being naturally inquisitive, began to look more carefully at the shop. It was full of tables and chairs, mostly rather battered and broken down, with thick layers of dust everywhere. It didn't seem to be very interesting and the dust made him want to sneeze, but just as he was about to go out again, he saw a mirror at the back of the shop. It hung in the gloom over a cracked, marble washstand. It was an oval mirror, rather old-fashioned, with a carved silver frame and handles at the sides. What had attracted his attention was the fact that he couldn't see anything in it at all. The glass was a strange dull green. He moved forward into the gloom to take a closer look. And, as he stared at it, he saw what appeared to be a mist, moving slowly over the surface. He put out his hand to touch it and the mist closed over his fingers. As he watched, an extraordinary thing happened. The mist began to swirl and coil itself over the glass and round the frame. Faster and faster it whirled and all the time it grew brighter and brighter. Wisps groped out like thin fingers into the dusty air. Sebastian watched in amazement as the wreaths of smoke twisted and writhed and slowly the mirror turned a pure, emerald green. In his astonishment, Sebastian leaned forward and touched the handles. At once the clouds of smoke were drawn into the mirror and slowly the green mist dissolved away. The mirror seemed to burn with a white light and then—most astonishing and unbelievable of all—the face of a young girl appeared before him. She looked about twelve years old. Long brown hair hung round her pale face. Her eyes were green and glistening with tears. Suddenly she looked up, and gave a start. She seemed to be staring straight at Sebastian. An expression of wonder and bewilderment came over her sad face, and she parted her lips to speak.

'Who are you?' said a little voice from far away.

Sebastian was so startled that he let go of the handles and took a step backwards. At once the mist began to close over the surface and he just caught a glimpse of the girl's face dissolving into tears before it vanished and the mirror became a sheet of dull green glass again.

Sebastian looked round quickly and saw the two men still talking as if nothing had happened. Everything in the shop was just as it had been when he came in. Had he been dreaming? He turned back to the mirror. There, clinging to the bottom of the frame was a large tear-drop. It fell into his outstretched hand and lay there, winking and sparkling like a diamond.

He made his way out of the shop and towards home as quickly as possible. He had completely lost all sense of time and was anxious not to be late. The snow had stopped falling now and most people were safely inside their houses, so he could walk very quickly and think undisturbed. He felt very angry with himself for letting go of the handles and the girl's unhappiness worried him. He couldn't begin to understand what was happening and wondered if he should tell anyone about it. He decided against it at last, partly because he knew they wouldn't believe him, and partly because the grown-ups in the shop had seen nothing and so probably Mrs Parkin and Sarah wouldn't either.

When he got home supper was ready on the table, so he rushed upstairs to change out of his wet clothes and went into the kitchen just as the clock was striking half past six. Mrs Parkin was taking some potatoes baked in their jackets out of the oven and the heat from the oven door had made her face even shinier than usual. A dish of yellow butter was beginning to melt and begged to be spread on the fluffy potatoes. Crisp, brown sausages nestled against chunks of pink ham, and a large apple pie, bursting with spices and currants, was waiting to take its applause on the kitchen table.

The warmth, and Mrs Parkin's good cooking, made Sebastian feel rather better about things and the girl's tear-stained, unhappy face began to fade from his mind. He was sitting comfortably by the fire, listening to Mrs Parkin's stories about the country, and the cottage in which she had lived as a child, when he happened to glance up to the shelf where all the silver was kept when it wasn't in use. The teapot grinned down at him, pink in the firelight, and then suddenly, quite unmistakably, a large tear fell from its silver eye, rolled down its bumpy metal cheek and landed splosh! on the toe of Sebastian's shoe.

Then Sebastian knew what he had to do. He must buy the mirror and see if the girl would appear again, and if she did, well, he would try to find a way to help her. For one thing was clear in this extraordinary situation, she needed help badly. Now that he had decided what to do, he wondered why it hadn't occurred to him before, for he felt very excited and filled with curiosity to know what was behind these mysterious happenings.

In bed that night, Sebastian dreamed of teapots and mirrors, and strange things which he couldn't explain, and just before he woke up, he dreamed that the girl with the green eyes and the long brown hair was running down the street towards him, laughing.

Next morning, as he sat doing Latin with his tutor, Mr Drycrust, the hours seemed to pass even more slowly than usual. At last, after clearing his throat for the fifty-second time, Mr Drycrust gave him the last sentence of his homework, and went creaking down the stairs to the front door. Sebastian had an hour before lunch, in which to find the shop again and buy the mirror. He had emptied his money-box and found that he had tenpence, which in those days was worth a lot more than it is now. Clutching the money in his pocket he went down to tell Mrs Parkin that he was going for a walk.

It was not quite as cold outside as the day before, and although the snow was still lying in patches on the ground, a pale wintry sun was struggling to show itself in the foggy sky. He managed to find his way quite easily to the narrow street where the shop was. Sitting on the doorstep of the shop was a large orange cat, rather thin but with a smooth glossy coat, and when it saw Sebastian approaching, it got up and stood by the door, waiting to be let in. Sebastian pushed the door open and he and the cat slipped inside. The cat began to purr very loudly and to rub itself against Sebastian's legs, and it was so strong and moved so rapidly that he had a job not to fall over in the tangle of paws and tail and whiskers around his feet. There was only one man in the shop, whom Sebastian hadn't seen before, and he watched with a smile as Sebastian struggled to sort himself out.

'What can I do for you, son?' he said.

'I'd like to buy a mirror, please,' said Sebastian. He was afraid that the man might think it odd if he said that he particularly wanted the one you couldn't see anything in.

'I'm afraid we're out of mirrors just now. Not much in demand at the moment you know,' the man said, looking genuinely sorry. At that, the cat walked to the back of the shop, jumped up on to the marble washstand below the mirror and sat there, purring loudly.

'Well, bless me,' said the man, 'that cat's got more sense than I have.'

The cat stared at the man with bright unwinking eyes.

'Will this one be all right, sonny? I'm afraid it needs a good clean. I'd quite forgotten we had it. I can't even remember anyone bringing it in, now I come to think of it, it just seems to have turned up, like the cat here, out of nowhere.'

A sudden thought came into Sebastian's head. Since yesterday some strange things had happened, and ordinary things suddenly seemed to have a life of their own. He looked at the cat. It got up at once, jumped down and came over to him, and then sat down squarely, right on Sebastian's toe. Sebastian had a feeling that he was going to meet the cat again.

'How much is the mirror?' he asked.

'Well, now, seeing it's so dirty, I think I'll only ask ten-pence for it. It's probably more than a hundred years old, and worth a lot more I should think, but then, not many people seem to want them at the moment.'

Sebastian handed over his tenpence and the man took the mirror down and wrapped it up.

'Here you are, son. I hope that's what you want.'

'Thank you very much,' said Sebastian and turned to go. 'By the way, how long has the cat been here?' he asked.

'Why bless me! He was here yesterday when I got back from my mother's. I left a couple of friends to look after the shop and it seems he just walked in a few minutes before I did, cool as you please, and took up residence on the washstand. Well, I've always been fond of animals and as it's nasty weather, I don't mind him staying here for a bit. I expect he'll wander off again in a few days' time.'

Sebastian felt sure now that the cat had something to do with the strange happenings. He thanked the man again and then went out into the daylight. As he walked down the narrow street towards home, he turned round for a moment to have a last look at the shop. He could just make out a pair of yellow eyes beaming at him from the dark, dusty window.

Sebastian climbed the stairs to the attic as quietly as possible. He knew that if Mrs Parkin or Sarah discovered that he'd spent all his pocket-money on an old mirror, he would have to do some explaining. There were three attic rooms at the top of the house and no one went up there more than once a year, so it was a wonderful place to hide things. Sebastian went to the attic right at the end, which was the largest and also the lightest room. There was a hook on one of the walls which was just the right height for the mirror, so he unwrapped it carefully and hung it up. Then he looked at it. Yes, the mist was there, moving slowly over the surface and somehow, in the attic, with the sun sending white shafts of light across the floor it seemed even more magical and mysterious. He went downstairs again to have his lunch.

Luckily Mrs Parkin and the others had already eaten so he could relax over his delicious steak-and-kidney pie, and also do his homework between mouthfuls. He knew it was important not to neglect this sort of thing as everyone would soon start wondering what he could be doing which didn't leave time for his homework. The last few lines of Latin were done over a fat, sticky, treacle pudding. Unfortunately a few blobs of treacle managed to find their way on to his exercise book, but he scraped them off as best he could, and then it was all finished. Mrs Parkin was having a quick nap in her room, Sarah was shopping, Sylvester was, as usual, sitting in his father's study poring over official papers and dull things like that, and William was exercising the horses. Sebastian felt that it was safe to go up to the attic and see if the mirror would work for him again.

Sebastian stood in front of the mirror and watched the mist as it groped its way over the surface in small circles. Nothing happened. He kept looking at it, a terrible feeling of disappointment creeping over him. After five minutes of standing without moving he was beginning to grow quite stiff, and he was just about to sit down on the old sagging sofa, which was one of his favourite sitting places when he felt unhappy, when he heard someone calling him. He rushed downstairs to be met by Sarah, who had just got back from her shopping. She had bought him a new pair of boots and wanted to see if they fitted. She was so busy chatting about the people she'd met in the shops that she didn't notice that he was unusually quiet and rather gloomy. Sebastian tried the boots on, told her that they fitted perfectly and then went upstairs to the attic again, hoping that if he was patient something might happen. Sure enough, the moment he entered the room he saw that the mirror was changing. The mist was moving very fast and already the room was quite thick with smoke. Then it occurred to him that perhaps the mirror had known that someone was going to call him, and had waited for a time

18

when it wouldn't be interrupted. It was now a bright emerald in colour so Sebastian, remembering the events of yesterday, took hold of the handles on either side of the mirror. There was a flash of burning, white light and then slowly the girl's face appeared. This time she saw him at once and before he could say anything she called out in her faint voice, 'Please don't go away. Please listen to me!'

Sebastian, feeling suddenly self-conscious, said that of course he wasn't going to go away and that he certainly wouldn't have gone to the trouble of buying the mirror if he hadn't meant to listen. It occurred to him that he might have sounded cross. He hadn't intended to be rude of course. He was fascinated and excited, but felt that it wouldn't be manly to show it, so it came out as crossness instead. However, she didn't seem to mind, for she smiled and said that of course it was silly of her. It was just that she was so glad to see him and that she had been waiting all morning, hoping that the mirror was going to work again. Sebastian said he was sorry and that if he had sounded cross it was just that it was all so surprising.

'Oh dear, yes, it must be,' said the girl. 'By the way, have you come across my cat Mantari?'

'Do you mean the cat that was in the shop?' asked Sebastian.

'Well, I don't know where he actually went,' replied the girl. 'All I know is that he went off somewhere yesterday and when he came back this morning he was very excited about something, and kept jumping up to the mirror and purring a lot so I knew that something had happened to it. And I guessed that it must be you, as the mirror's never worked for anyone before. I've spent hours and days and weeks and years sitting in front of it, just hoping, but nothing ever happened until yesterday. You see, Mantari can get into your world. It's only me that can't.'

And with that she looked so sad that Sebastian was afraid she was going to cry.

'Look here,' he said hurriedly, 'why don't you tell me what this is all about. I really don't understand what's going on, but I promise that I'll do anything I can to help you.' He saw with relief that she was looking more cheerful again.

'Come on, now. Do tell me,' and he smiled encouragingly.

She gave him a little smile in return. 'I don't have time to tell you the whole story now. The mirror only works for a little while and then it fades and it won't work again until tomorrow. I have an idea though. You must come into my world. There is no time here so we can talk for hours and you'll only be gone from your world a few minutes.'

Sebastian felt this was all most confusing. 'This is all very well,' he said, 'but how do I find your world for a start?'

'That's easy,' she replied. 'Your Power Object will get you here.'

'Power Object?' said Sebastian, quite baffled.

'Well, you must have one or the mirror wouldn't have worked for you. It's all in the Book you know,' as if that explained everything. 'Quickly, think now. It's not likely to be the Emerald and it certainly can't be the Rose. We've got all the Mirror now—so it must be the Teapot.'

'Of course,' said Sebastian excitedly, 'the teapot! It's downstairs in the kitchen!'

'Wonderful,' she said. 'The Teapot will get you here then. By the way, what's your name? Quickly, the Mirror's beginning to fade!'

'Sebastian,' he shouted, and then the mist started to swirl over the mirror and the girl vanished. The attic room suddenly felt empty and cold. He let go of the handles and watched the marks on his hands disappear. Well, he was in it now and no mistake.

He felt excited and bewildered. What on earth could be the explanation for all this! It seemed just like a dream. He looked at the Mirror again to make sure that this extraordinary adventure was really happening to him. It hung there in the silent attic, the mist hovering over the silver frame. He decided to go downstairs to have a good look at the Teapot, and wait to see what would happen next. Just as he was half-way down, Sarah called up from the kitchen to ask him if he would run an errand for her. 'Bother!' thought Sebastian, 'this might spoil everything.' He rushed down, hoping desperately that it wouldn't take too long.

'Ah, Sebastian,' said Sarah, as he went into the kitchen, 'be a good chap and take the teapot to be mended for me. The hinge on the lid has got broken somehow and there'll be an awful to-do if the lid gets lost. Just pop into a cab and take it down to Mr Eldritch. He'll fix it in a moment.'

'All right,' said Sebastian, and took the money she gave him, thinking that perhaps the teapot wouldn't work anyway if it was broken, so it was just as well. He took his muffler from the hall and went out into the street.

There was a hansom cab just outside the front door, so he told the cabby where he wanted to go and climbed in, holding the Teapot. They set off at quite a pace and Sebastian was enjoying himself, curled up against the padded seat, and listening to the horse's hooves clattering over the cobbled streets. He looked at the Teapot. Apart from its broken lid it was just the same as usual. Then he began to think that perhaps the cabby had got lost, for they had been travelling for rather a long time and he knew that it wasn't all that far to the mender's. Suddenly he noticed that they were gathering speed and to judge from the sound of the hooves they were no longer on cobbles. He knelt up on the seat to look out of the window and saw, to his astonishment, the hedges, trees and fields of deep countryside.

Sebastian knew that the country was a long way from the centre of London where he lived. He leaned out of the window to ask the cabby where on earth he was going, and then nearly fell out of it in his surprise. There was no sign of the cabby but there, sitting on the driver's seat, his ears flattened to the wind, was the orange cat. The Teapot had found a way after all.

Sebastian's heart began to beat quickly, but he was not afraid. He peered out of the window and saw that the trees and hedges were growing more and more thickly and at times they tangled together over the road to form a tunnel. At these points it was very dark indeed and no one could have blamed him if he had felt just a little nervous.

At last they began to slow down and Sebastian saw in the distance, jutting up from the trees, the pointed turrets of what appeared to be a very large house. He hugged the Teapot closer to him and tried to ignore his thumping heart. A sudden bend in the road brought them up to a gate. It was very high and made of a sort of iron, which had been twisted to form the shapes of flowers and animals. In the sunlight it would probably have been very beautiful. In the twilight it seemed rather sinister. The cat jumped down from its seat and stalked over to the gate. It rubbed itself against the iron beasts and flowers and at once the gate split silently down the middle and the two halves swung back. The cat jumped back on to the box and the carriage moved forward. The drive was much wider than the road which led up to it, and on either side was a garden which was dark and overgrown. A small stream wound through the bushes, and he could hear it murmuring over the stones and trickling into shallow basins. The trees weren't like any he had seen before. Some were very spiky and black and he could see the light glinting on large and needle-sharp thorns. Some had branches which were

wrapped tightly round their trunks and the ends of the branches looked almost like hands. Another leaned across the stream and trailed its long branches over the water as if loath to let it pass.

Then Sebastian heard the sound of gravel under the carriage wheels and, as they swung round a corner, the largest house he had ever seen came into view. It was built of stone, and round the hundreds of windows someone had carved an intricate pattern of fruits, vines and leaves. Most of the windows were dark and the tall towers frowned down on him threateningly. Sebastian climbed out of the carriage, still holding the Teapot, and looked for the cat. While he had been staring at the house, the cat must have slipped away. There was no sign of it, or any other living thing. Everything was silent. He walked up the steps to the huge front door. It opened slowly before him. He almost gasped. Before him lay a long corridor which ran as far as the eye could see, and it was lit by a blaze of candles. Hundreds and thousands of them hung in great clusters on the wall. Some of them bent out from their holders and dripped slowly on to the floor. Yellow heaps of wax rose up on either side, twisted into shapes which looked like stumpy little people crouching in the shadows. Sebastian walked forward and the door closed behind him. This made him feel uneasy but there was little he could do but go on. The smoke from the candles hung in heavy blue wisps above his head. The smell of the wax was strong and made the corridor stuffy. He walked along, stepping quickly in and out of the shadows and brushing off the drips which fell on his clothes. When he reached the end of the corridor he found that another ran across it, exactly like the first. He realized that if he wasn't very careful he would get hopelessly lost. As he stood still, wondering in which direction he ought to go, something warm and furry rubbed itself against his legs. It was the cat.

'Hello, puss!' said Sebastian. He was glad that his voice sounded firm and quite ordinary.

The cat set off quickly along the corridor and Sebastian followed him. He found it rather difficult to keep up, for the cat obviously knew the way so well that it never paused for a moment. At one moment the cat vanished out of sight round a corner and Sebastian began to run, for the thought of being lost in these endless, twisting corridors was terrifying. However as he came panting round the corner the cat was sitting waiting for him with a pitying expression on his face as if to say, 'I suppose you can't help being a poor slow human.' His dignity was rather spoiled when a large blob of wax fell from a candle above his head and landed right between his ears. Sebastian very much wanted to laugh but felt it would be unkind. The cat shook his head rather crossly and they went on, this time more slowly.

At last they came to a small wooden door, set deep in the wall, which seemed to be the end of their journey. 'Please come in,' said a voice from the other side of the door. Sebastian recognized it as belonging to the girl in the mirror, but this time it sounded much nearer. He opened the door and slipped inside, the cat following at his heels.

He found himself in a very large room. There were a great many windows along two of its walls, so only a few candles were burning, which was a great relief to the eyes after the glare of the corridors. He looked around him in silence, quite overawed by what he saw.

The walls were hung with a silver shimmering cloth which sparkled as it caught the light, and the long curtains and the marble floor were pale gold. There was a bright fire crackling in a silver grate and in front of it was a sofa and a silver table of exquisite beauty. The sofa was piled with deep gold, velvet cushions. On one wall hung an oval mirror with a silver frame. Its glass was green and it looked just like the one which was hanging in the attic in London.

Sitting on the window seat was the girl he had seen in the mirror. She wore a vivid crimson dress which fell in graceful folds around her feet and shone out among the pale shimmering colours of the room. The orange cat was sitting on her knee, purring loudly, and they both looked at him expectantly.

'Hallo,' she said at last, smiling, but seeming just a little shy. 'Do come and sit down.'

Sebastian went over to the window seat and sat down beside her. They looked at each other for a moment. It was

rather difficult to know what to say next. Then the cat
stepped on to Sebastian's lap and carefully chewed off one
of his buttons. They both laughed and at once the shyness
went and they felt almost like old friends. The cat spat the
button out on to the floor, jumped down and began to
play an elaborate game with it, which the children watched
with amusement.

'Well,' said Sebastian, 'I'm here. The Teapot worked
very quickly. It's all jolly weird though and I'm dying to
know what's going on. By the way, what's your name?'

The girl thought for a moment and then she remembered. 'It's Melissa. I had a struggle to remember it just now, because you're the first person I've seen for nearly a hundred years, except Mantari, of course, and as he can't talk of course, I haven't needed a name.'

'A hundred years?' said Sebastian, astounded. 'Look, you'd better start from the beginning and tell me everything.'

'All right,' said Melissa, 'but first of all, would you like something to eat?'

'Rather!' said Sebastian, 'lunch seems hours ago.'

'Very well,' she said, 'you can have anything you like.'

'Do you mean that? It won't be any bother or anything?' he added politely.

Melissa laughed. 'No bother at all, I assure you.'

'Well, in that case, I'd like toast and honey please and some cake if you've got it. I suppose you wouldn't happen to have some gingerbread?'

Sebastian watched as Melissa went over to the silver table and spoke to it.

'I'd like tea for two, please, with toast and honey, and one of your delicious chocolate cakes, and some fresh gingerbread. Oh, and could we have a saucer of milk and a plate of sardines for Mantari, please? You have to be polite to it,' she explained to Sebastian, 'otherwise it gets cross, and the toast arrives burnt and there are bugs in the cake or something.'

Sebastian looked at the table and there, spread on a green embroidered cloth was everything they had asked for. It had appeared quite suddenly out of nowhere. They sat down to tea at once. Sebastian really enjoyed himself for it all tasted quite delicious. Mantari ate noisily and was evidently hungry as well. Melissa was the only one who didn't eat much.

'I had something to eat before you came,' she explained,

28

'I got terribly restless waiting for you to arrive so I had to do something to pass the time. Do you feel better now?'

'Much,' said Sebastian as he wiped the last few crumbs from his mouth. 'That was jolly good. Thanks very much. Now, supposing we get down to business and you tell me what this is all about? By the way, are you quite sure they won't be missing me at home?'

'Oh yes,' said Melissa, 'don't worry. It's all in the Book. I've had nearly a hundred years to read it and it explains quite clearly about this time thing. A day here is no time at all in your world.'

'So in fact,' said Sebastian, 'you haven't grown any older in the hundred years you've been here. There is simply no time here at all.'

'Right,' said Melissa, 'it's not going to be quite as difficult to explain as I thought. I'll start from the beginning, shall I?'

They settled back comfortably on the sofa and the cat curled up on Melissa's knee. Then she cleared her throat and began.

I was born in India one hundred and eleven years ago. As I've been here ninety-nine years, that makes me twelve years old. My mother and father I can't remember at all. A few months after I was born, the little colony in which we lived was invaded by a tribe of bandits and my parents were killed with many others. An Englishman and I were the only survivors. This man felt sorry for me and so, rather than leave me to the wild animals, he decided to look after me until he could get back to England and find my relatives. However the colony was in a wild and desolate part of India and there were no towns for many hundreds of miles. The bandits had taken all the horses and so the man had no choice but to set out on foot and make for the coast where we could be picked up by a passing boat. He travelled for many days through the dark jungle, carrying me in his arms. Soon the little food he had found in the colony, left behind by the bandits, ran out. He met nothing but snakes and lizards and wild birds, no food or water anywhere and no sign of the coast. At last, weak from hunger and thirst, he began to grow feverish and he lost all sense of direction. He forced himself to go on, although he had by now given up all hope of staying alive for more than a few days, and suddenly he came into a clearing. A spring of sparkling water bubbled through it and trees hung over the pool, laden with ripe fruit. He summoned up enough energy to eat and drink and to feed me as best he could, although he didn't think either of us would survive much longer, and then, taking me in his arms, he lay down beneath a tree and fell asleep. He woke suddenly to find that the tree under which we had slept had twined its branches around us, and no matter how hard he struggled, he couldn't break the knotted arms.

While he lay there, trying to think of how he could escape, a shadow fell across the clearing, and looking up, he saw, standing over him, the tallest man he had ever seen. His skin was white as snow and he was dressed from head to foot in a robe of sapphires and amethysts, which cast a bright light on the water. His slippers were made of diamonds and on one finger he wore a ring, set with an enormous ruby. He stared down at the trapped man and his eyes were ablaze with evil. Under his gaze the weary traveller felt his body grow cold as ice and he clutched me closer to him and prepared for death. However the stranger spoke. 'You have eaten the Fruit of Wealth and drunk the Waters of Misery. It would not benefit me to kill you. I shall release you from the tree on one condition. That in twelve years' time, when you are one of the richest men in your country, you will give me the thing that you love above all else for my Treasure House. You will never see it again for my Treasure House is not in your world or in

your time, nor will you ever see me again after that time.'
The poor man thought that he was either dreaming or
dying, so he agreed readily. At once the branches of the
tree fell away, and the stranger vanished. The bewildered
man got up and began walking immediately, and within a
few hours we reached the coast. We were sighted by a passing cargo ship on its way to the Orient. They took us
aboard and treated us very kindly. Within six months we
were back in England and a search was begun for my
relatives. It was unsuccessful, but by this time the man
had grown to love me so he was overjoyed when the
authorities agreed that he should become my guardian.

While he had been in India, his great-uncle had died and
left him a large inheritance. So, after the papers for my
adoption had been signed, we moved to London. With the
money from his inheritance he bought a fleet of merchant
ships and grew very rich. He was a very kind man and no
one could have had a better father. We were very happy
together and I loved him dearly. He used to tell me about
all the adventures he had had in his earlier life and we
spent many happy hours together laughing over the funny
things he had seen and heard. But it seemed at times that
all the warmth and happiness would suddenly leave him.
He would sit beside me, staring in front of him, and looking
so sad that I could hardly bear it. I always asked him what
was troubling him but he would never tell me. He had
terrible dreams too, I often heard him cry out during the
night. He had only told me, you see, how my parents had
died, and how we had been rescued after many days walking through the jungle. Of the rest I knew nothing. One
day, when I was about ten years old, and he had fallen into
one of these silent, unhappy moods I begged him to tell me
what made him so sad. I pleaded so strongly with him that
at last he gave way and told me the strange story which I
have just related. He seemed to be happier after he had

told it and I, like him, thought that it was just a dream, the wanderings of a fatigued and feverish mind. We never mentioned it to each other again and I noticed that my guardian's moods became fewer and fewer and he no longer cried out in the night. However, a few months after my twelfth birthday, as we were sitting round the fire one night, a terrifying thing happened. The fire began to roar and great flames leapt up the chimney as if a violent gust of wind had passed through the room. We turned round in alarm and there, standing behind us, was the man my guardian had met in the forest exactly twelve years before. He was just as my guardian had described him. The huge ruby on his finger glinted in the firelight. He spoke, and his voice filled me with terror.

'I have come as I promised. Give me whatever you love most in the world and your part in the bargain will be complete. Do not attempt to deceive me for I shall be sure to find you out. You will see that anything I touch will lose its value if you do not treasure it above all else.'

My guardian got up at once and went over to his desk. He pressed a hidden spring and opened a secret drawer. He brought out a huge and beautiful diamond, which winked and glowed and almost diminished the glory of the stranger's ruby.

'Take this,' said my guardian, 'it is the most beautiful and valuable thing I possess,' and he gave it to the stranger.

But as the stranger took it, its radiance faded and it became a mere rock in his hands. The stranger was angry.

'I give you one more chance. Bring me whatever you value more dearly than life itself or I shall kill you and the child and this house will be burnt to the ground.'

At that my guardian cried out, 'Oh spare the child, I beg you! Kill me, take everything I own, but do not harm Melissa!'

The stranger flew into a rage. 'I have been tricked! I see it is the child that you love above all else. Very well, I shall take her, and the prophecy of the Waters of Misery shall be fulfilled.'

My guardian went down on his knees and implored him to be merciful but the stranger laughed at him and took me by the wrist. Suddenly the room and my guardian vanished and I was whirling in darkness. I could feel the harsh grip on my arm, which grew tighter and tighter until I lost consciousness. I woke up to find myself in this house. I was lying on a bed in a room so magnificent that I could hardly believe my eyes. The stranger was standing at the foot of the bed and when he saw that I was awake, he spoke to me in a voice as cold as steel.

'You will remain in this house for ever. There is no time here. You will never grow older than you are. I shall visit here once a year to see my treasures and apart from that you will never see another living soul.'

Melissa sighed heavily and Sebastian didn't know what to say. It was all too astounding to take in at once. The cat wriggled on Melissa's lap and looked at the children as they stared at one another in silence.

'Well,' said Sebastian at last, 'so what did you do then? It must have been jolly difficult to think of things to do for a hundred years.'

Melissa sighed again. 'It was. At first I could only think of my guardian and how miserable he must have been.'

'What do you think happened to him?' asked Sebastian.

'To tell you the truth,' said Melissa, 'I've never been able to quite work that out. As there is no time here, if I ever escaped from this world and went into yours again, I should go back to the time when I left it. In fact it would be about ninety years before you were born!'

This was such a strange thought that it took Sebastian some time to take it in.

33

'If that is the case,' said Sebastian slowly, 'then we could never meet in the ordinary world because in my time you'd be—well, I suppose you—well, its very likely that you'd be...'

'Dead,' nodded Melissa. 'It is rather an extraordinary idea, isn't it. So really I'm already history!'

'I say,' said Sebastian, 'this means that whatever happens now, that is, if we manage to get you out of here, and I jolly well think we will,' he added hastily, for Melissa was beginning to look forlorn and rather despairing, 'it is going to change the past.'

'Exactly,' said Melissa, 'if I escape, then I go back to the time when my guardian and I were sitting round the fire and everything will go on as if none of this had ever happened. If I don't manage to escape,' here her chin wobbled slightly but she managed not to give way, 'then my guardian will have lived on alone without me until his death, and the prophecy of the Waters will have been fulfilled.' Here a large tear-drop fell on to the table in front of them. A loud hissing sound and a puff of green smoke as it landed, made them jump.

'Gosh,' said Sebastian, when they'd all recovered from the shock, 'I can hardly believe this is all happening. I keep expecting to wake up. Supposing you tell me now how we can get you out of here. You did say something about everything being in a book when we were talking through the mirror earlier on.'

'Yes, that's right,' said Melissa, 'I think it would be a good idea if we went and had a look at it. I'll just clear away the tea things.'

She wiped her eyes with the folds of her crimson dress and spoke to the table. 'We all enjoyed our tea very much, thank you. Please be kind enough to clear it away now.'

At once the things on the table disappeared and a small piece of paper appeared there instead. Sebastian picked it up and then started to laugh. 'Why, it's trying to charge us a shilling for the tea!'

'It's only showing off,' said Melissa, 'take it back at once, table, and don't be so silly. You know I haven't got any money anyway. Come on, Sebastian, let's go and see the Book before the table gets really annoying!'

Mantari uncurled himself and jumped down to lead the way.

'I say,' said Melissa, 'I don't want to sound silly or anything but it is nice to have someone to talk to after all these years.'

Sebastian nodded. 'Actually you do look much better,' he said, 'less red around the eyes and not so pale.'

He didn't mean to be rude, in fact he meant it as a compliment and Melissa, after a moment's thought, decided to take it as one. She gave him a happy smile and they went out into the corridor.

The air seemed even thicker with candle smoke than before and bits of wax clung to the hem of Melissa's dress as it trailed over the floor. Mantari walked ahead, glancing up nervously from time to time at the large blobs of hot wax which hung trembling above his head. They walked through miles of twisting corridors until they came to a door made of heavy oak and studded with nails. It was quite difficult to get it open. Sebastian had to give it a strong shove before it gave way and swung back noisily. The room they entered was dark and rather gloomy. Melissa went over to the empty grate of the fireplace and ordered the fire to burn, which it did with a great deal of crackling and spitting.

'Do all the things work in this house when you tell them to?' asked Sebastian, highly delighted with the idea.

'Oh yes,' said Melissa, 'I found that out the day I arrived. I was talking to myself, you see, and all these things kept appearing when I mentioned them, so I soon got the idea. The only thing which doesn't work for me is the gate. I've tried and tried being polite to it but it doesn't move. I once got the cat to open it for me but as soon as I went near it, it shut again before I had time to get through. There are enormous high walls all round the garden and they're terribly slippery. Its quite impossible to climb them. It seems that the only way for me to get out of

here is to destroy the magic. And that's where the Book
will help us. A few weeks after I arrived here, I was trying
to keep myself from being bored, so I began to explore this
end of the house. When I found this room I was terribly
pleased as I've always liked reading.'

Sebastian looked around him and saw in the glow from
the fire that the room was in fact a library. From floor to
ceiling were shelves absolutely stuffed with books, all
bound in leather of various colours. In front of the fire was
a high-backed settee. Sebastian sat down on it and Mantari jumped up beside him. Melissa walked up and down
the room, her dress rustling on the ground, and continued
her story.

'I began to look through the books, starting from the
bottom shelf and working upwards, but to my disappointment most of them were in languages I didn't understand

and all the ones I could find in English were very boring. I decided to play a silly game, you know what it's like if you haven't anything to do, so I was going to close my eyes and just pick out any one to look at. Well, I had my eyes shut, and I was running my fingers along the backs of those books over there, when I felt one which was warm. All the others on either side were quite cold. I opened my eyes and felt it again. I hadn't imagined it. It felt quite different from the others. Look, I'll show you.'

She got up and went over to the wall opposite the fire-place. She stretched up to the shelf just above her head and felt the books carefully. Then she pulled one out and brought it over to Sebastian. It was bound in green leather and covered in strange signs, stamped in silver. As Melissa had said, it was warm and, when Sebastian opened it, wisps of greenish smoke floated up from the pages. He looked at the words on the first page but it was difficult to read them as the letters seemed to wriggle and dance about under his eyes.

'Its very hard to read, isn't it?' said Melissa, 'the letters do move around so.'

Sebastian managed to pin down the wriggling letters at last and read, THE BOOK OF THE ENCHANTER, WHEREIN LIES THE SECRET POWER OF ALL THINGS LIVING AND OTHERWISE, KNOWN AND UNKNOWN.

The Book trembled in his hands, and Sebastian felt rather like trembling too, for he realized that he was holding something that was magic, powerful, very precious and probably extremely dangerous as well. Melissa leaned over his shoulder and turned the pages until she came to a chapter about half-way through.

'This is the bit which concerns us. Shall I read it to you? I've had a lot of practice at it.' Sebastian nodded and Melissa began.

' "Chapter One Hundred and Fifty. 'The Treasure

House.' This is the secret of the Enchanter's power. The source of his strength is the Well, which lies in the bottommost chamber of the Treasure House. He who desires to break the Enchanter's power can only do so by uniting the Power Objects and taking them to the Well of the Enchanter. He must throw them into the Well, and he must then throw himself in afterwards or perish in the holocaust which will follow." '

'What's a holocaust?' interrupted Sebastian.

'I'm not sure,' said Melissa, 'I think it's a sort of upheaval or something. Anyway we'll find out if we ever get that far.'

Sebastian wasn't very keen on the idea of throwing himself into a well, but it was rather too late now to turn back. Anyway he couldn't possibly leave Melissa imprisoned in the Treasure House forever, now that he knew about it, without at least trying to help her.

'What are these Power Objects then?' he said.

'Well, that's all explained in another chapter,' she replied, and taking the Book on her knee, she turned back the pages until she came to a chapter near the beginning. 'I'll read it to you. "Chapter Seventy. The Power Objects. They are five in number. The magic of the Well is divided between them. In order of power they are: The Silver Fish, the Silver Teapot, the Silver Mirror, the Emerald and the Enchanter's Rose. In order to prevent the breaking of the Enchanter's power, the first four are scattered in different countries and different worlds. The fifth, the green Rose, grows in the garden of the Enchanter's Realm. The Power Objects are drawn towards each other and towards the Treasure House when their power is used for evil. Therefore if a good heart desires to end evil, it will find assistance in them." '

'Well,' said Sebastian slowly, 'what we have to do is to find these Power Objects, throw them into the Well and then you're free. We've already got the Teapot and the Mirror and as the Book says that the Objects are drawn here when the magic is used for evil, it shouldn't be too hard to find the others.'

'I suppose it isn't really as difficult as it sounds,' said Melissa, encouraged by Sebastian's cheerful tone. 'And, what's more, I think that we may already have another of them. I'm not sure and I could well be wrong, but it's the only explanation I can think of. You remember I told you that the Enchanter said I would never see another living soul? In that case how do you explain Mantari? I found him in the garden after I'd been here about a month. He was awfully thin and bedraggled and he'd obviously come a long way. As you can imagine, I was very pleased to see him. I fed him and cared for him and he soon got better. I don't know what it would have been like without him all that time. I would have gone mad with loneliness.' Here Mantari stretched up his paw and patted Melissa's face. 'Anyway, the fact that Mantari found his way here and has lived for about eight times as long as cats normally do, can mean only one thing, don't you think?'

For a moment Sebastian didn't understand. What did all this have to do with the Power Objects? Then it dawned upon him. Of course, the Silver Fish! What could be more natural than for a cat to eat a fish. And if that fish happened to possess magic powers the cat would perhaps absorb those powers itself. 'You think that Mantari has eaten the Silver Fish?' he asked Melissa.

'Well, it does seem a very good explanation to me,' she replied, 'it would explain how he got here because of the thing about the Objects being drawn to the Treasure House, and having legs it would be the simplest thing in the world for the magic in him to send him here. He must have *some* magic, the Enchanter is too clever to make a mistake and he was quite definite about me being completely alone. It's only a guess of course, but I've had ninety-nine years to think about it and I've never been able to come up with any other explanation. What do you think?'

'I think you may well be right,' said Sebastian, 'but what worries me is that if we take it that this idea is correct and we throw everything into the Well and it doesn't happen to be right after all, we shall have ruined our chances for good. I think you'd better choose whether we decide to take that risk or not.'

Melissa thought about it for a moment, and then said, 'I think we should go ahead and look for the other two Objects and consider that we already have the Fish. It's nearly time for the Enchanter to come and I'm a bit worried that he might suspect something. I think that we ought to be as quick as possible, don't you?'

'Right then,' he agreed. 'Now the thing is to get the Emerald.'

They looked blankly at one another. It might be in any country in any world. It was going to be more difficult than he had at first thought. 'Well,' he said at last, 'if we're going to get anywhere it will have to be with the help of magic. At least they're on our side, for there's no doubt about the Enchanter being evil. No one who was good would keep someone a prisoner forever just out of revenge.'

As he said that, the Book jumped right out of his hands and landed on the floor with a crash. The pages fluttered over and over until they came to the last but one chapter of the Book. Great streams of smoke poured up into the dank air of the room. Then it calmed down, and Sebastian picked it up carefully.

'I say,' said Melissa looking at the Book over his shoulder, 'I've never seen that chapter before. I'm sure it wasn't there last time I looked through it. How strange!'

'It obviously understood what I was saying,' said

Sebastian, very excited, 'and is going to help us.' The Book sent up a little puff of smoke, as if to agree. 'Can you read what it says?'

' "Chapter Three Hundred and Ninety-four," ' read Melissa aloud. ' "The Summoning of the Elements—Fire, Water, Wind and Earthquake." ' Well, I suppose one of these can help us find the Emerald. Which one though?'

'I can't see that Fire or Earthquake would be much good,' said Sebastian, 'try Water and Wind first.'

Melissa turned over the page and read to herself the part headed 'To Summon the Water'. After a few seconds she looked up in dismay. 'This is no good at all. You have to say the poem which is written at the bottom of the page, while you're holding a Power Object. Well that's all right, but it has to be done at the time when the sun is highest in the sky, and from the middle of an ocean!'

'That sounds impossibly difficult,' agreed Sebastian. 'The only oceans I know are enormous, and it would take days to get to the middle of them. Anyway I couldn't afford it and Mrs Parkin would just laugh at me if I suggested going. We'd better have a look at summoning the Wind.'

Melissa turned over another page and found the part about the Wind. She read for a moment and then looked up excitedly. 'This is better. There's another poem you have to say while holding a Power Object and you have to say it at midnight, standing on the highest place you can find. Oh, and it has to be a night when there's a new moon, and with your eyes shut. I think that sounds much more possible, don't you?'

'I don't see why we couldn't manage that,' said Sebastian.

'Wait a minute though,' said Melissa, looking suddenly distressed, 'I'd quite forgotten. It says that it has to be on the night of a new moon. Well, there is no moon here! No stars, no sun, nothing! Just night and day. I can't get out of here to a world which does have a moon, and the spell won't work without it. Oh dear, and just as I was beginning to feel quite hopeful.' She turned her head away and Sebastian knew it was because she was feeling close to tears again.

'Well in that case,' said Sebastian hurriedly, 'I suggest that I should go and look for the Emerald alone. There's no reason why the spell shouldn't work in the ordinary world and there's definitely a moon there!'

'Sebastian, would you really do that,' said Melissa looking at him with shining eyes, 'that would be very brave.'

'Oh, nonsense,' said Sebastian, sounding much more courageous than he felt. 'It's the only thing we can do. And anyway, it might be dangerous, not at all the sort of thing for a girl.'

Melissa, for a moment, felt rather cross at the suggestion that a girl wasn't any good in a dangerous situation, and almost started an argument, but she remembered in time that it was very good of Sebastian to help her and it was silly to risk spoiling things just for the sake of pride.

'You're probably quite right,' she said, 'and I think it's jolly good of you to do so much just for a girl.'

Sebastian looked at her, a little puzzled for a moment, and then he understood. He grinned at her in such a teasing way that she had to laugh too, and they were firm friends from that moment onwards.

'Let's have a look at the poem,' he said turning back to the Book. He managed to keep the wriggling letters in their places for just long enough to read the poem, which went like this:

> O Wind, Father of the Sky,
> Gather your gentle Zephyrs
> And rough Northern blasts.

43

By the Power of all Things
Living and Otherwise, Known and Unknown,
I call thee, O Maker of Storms,
O Maker of soft Breezes,
Give me audience, O Master,
O Wind, Hear my call.

'It says in the Book that you have to have your eyes shut while you're saying it so obviously you'll have to learn it off by heart,' said Melissa. 'Do you think you could manage that?'

'I should think so,' replied Sebastian, 'have you got a piece of paper so I can write it down?'

Melissa thought for a moment. 'Oh yes, of course. There's a writing-desk in my bedroom. We can ask it for a pencil and some paper. We'll have to leave the Book here though. I've tried before to take it out of here, but there's some sort of magic which makes it impossible to get it through the door, a kind of invisible barrier. Are you going to come with me?'

'All right,' said Sebastian, 'you lead the way.'

But Mantari had already jumped down and was waiting by the door. He obviously considered that it was his job to show the way through the twisting corridors. They set off and pretty soon they came to a broad stone staircase. At the top was a tiny door made of silver oak.

'I wish there was some oil for this door,' said Melissa, as she opened it, 'it's got such an awful squeak.'

Just as she spoke a large can of oil, like the sort you use for bicycles, appeared at her feet and there was a great scramble as they all fell over it and each other. 'Bother,' said Melissa as she picked herself up. 'You really have to think before you say anything in this house. It can be very annoying at times.'

When they had sorted themselves out, Sebastian took a

look at the room. It was breath-takingly beautiful. Right in the centre of the room was an enormous bed with a silver canopy. Hanging down from it were curtains of a gorgeous deep rose pink and the coverlet was made of tiny pieces of mother-of-pearl sewn together with silver thread. Apart from the little writing desk and a small silver chair there was no other furniture, but all over the walls, from floor to ceiling, grew clusters of white flowers, smothering the grey stone-work and filling the room with a delicate and mysterious scent. The floor was grey marble and looked almost like glass, it was so highly polished.

'Do the flowers ever die?' asked Sebastian, as he gently touched the frail petals.

'Oh, no,' said Melissa. 'Because there is no time here, everything always stays the same. Things don't get dirty either. I've worn this dress all the time I've been here, and it's just as it was when I found it lying on the bed, my first day here. It was such a lovely colour I couldn't resist trying it on, and as soon as I had it on, all my other clothes just vanished and I haven't seen them since. It does save a lot of trouble, although sometimes I've wished things would get a little dirty just to give me something to do. Oh well, we'd better get on with the poem, I suppose. It's getting late and I'm feeling rather sleepy after all this excitement.'

And she did look tired. There were dark shadows under her eyes and she looked very pale. 'We'd like some writing paper and a pencil, please,' said Melissa, and they appeared in a trice.

'Let's go down and copy the poem out, then,' said Sebastian, 'I'm beginning to feel quite tired too, and I've got to get back home and stay awake through a whole afternoon yet.'

It was a very strange thought indeed. They went down to the Room of Books and the poem was soon written out, and then all that was left to do was to say goodbye.

Melissa was beginning to yawn at least every three minutes and even Mantari was blinking sleepily.

'Right,' said Sebastian, 'I shall go home and learn the poem as quickly as I can, and find out when the next new moon is. Then I'll come and tell you, through the Mirror, shall I? I expect you'd like to know what's going on.'

'Oh yes,' said Melissa, 'please do. There are so many things I want to ask you anyway, like how you found the Mirror and what London is like now, and where you live and about your family. We've really hardly begun to know each other. I wish I wasn't so sleepy.' And here she gave another vast yawn and her eyelids drooped.

'Come on,' said Sebastian, 'I must go. Where's the Teapot? I mustn't forget that!'

'Here it is,' said Melissa, handing it to him, 'I'll come down to the front door with you.'

Sebastian said that she ought to go straight to bed and that he would be perfectly all right with Mantari to show him the way but when she pointed out that Mantari had slipped away and was nowhere to be found, he had to agree to her coming with him, as he could never have found the way himself. As they walked together through the silent corridors, neither of them said much but both were deep in thought. Sebastian was thinking, 'I do hope this turns out all right. It's a very weird thing to get mixed up in. I suppose I could possibly be dreaming but the girl seems quite real. I hope she won't be too disappointed if we don't manage to break the magic. Poor girl, fancy being shut up alone for a hundred years...'

And Melissa was thinking, 'I wonder what this boy thinks of all this. It must seem very strange to him. It's very kind of him to help me and I think he has a nice smile. Supposing we managed to break the magic, oh, just supposing I could get free...'

At this point they reached the front door, and it swung

46

open before them to reveal the hansom cab standing outside on the gravel. Mantari was sitting waiting for him on the driving seat and his eyes cast out two great beams of yellow light into the darkness. Sebastian saw that as Melissa had said, there were no stars and no moon. It made the night look very black indeed.

The children said goodbye to each other and each was suddenly seized with a feeling of sadness at parting. Neither of them could have explained why, after all they hardly knew each other. 'Rot!' thought Sebastian to himself, 'she'll be all right here alone. If she's managed for the last ninety-nine years she can manage for the next few days at least,' and as if to assure him of this, Melissa took him by the hand and said with a quiet, happy smile, 'Goodbye Sebastian. Thank you for coming and, well, thanks for everything. I shall sleep really well tonight, and I'll be waiting by the Mirror for you tomorrow. Have a good journey home.'

Sebastian climbed into the carriage and at once the wheels began to turn and they started down the long drive. Looking back, Sebastian just caught a glimpse of Melissa's crimson dress in the shaft of light from the open door, and then the carriage turned a corner and he was in complete darkness. He settled back in his seat and listened to the sound of the gravel crunching under the wheels. Then the carriage slowed down and stopped and Sebastian guessed that they were at the gate. After a few moments they rolled forward again and started to gather speed. Faster and faster and...Sebastian, quite worn out with the strange happenings of the day, fell fast asleep.

'Wake up, sonny. Come along now, wake up.'

Someone was shaking him. Sebastian opened his eyes and saw the round, red whiskery face of the cabby bending over him.

47

'Come on sonny,' said the cabby. 'We're here. Dropped off for forty winks did you? It's all play and no work for some of us.' He chuckled as Sebastian rubbed his eyes and peered out of the cab door which was standing open. There they were, outside his house in London, and it was broad daylight. He looked at the Teapot. There was no sign of a broken hinge, it was as good as new. He climbed out and paid the cabby. The fare was exactly the amount he had in his pocket, and he was sure that there was less money there than he had started with. 'This magic certainly thinks of everything,' he said to himself as he went into the house. Down in the kitchen Sarah was laying the tray for tea.

'Bless you, that was quick,' she said as she took the Teapot from him, 'My, Mr Eldritch has made a good job of this. Would you like your tea down here or shall I take it up to the library?'

Sebastian thought for a moment. He felt wide awake now. If he went up to the library he could start learning the poem straight away. He patted his pocket and, sure enough, there was an answering rustle of paper.

'I'll take it up, don't worry,' he said.

'All right,' said Sarah, 'I think the fire's already been lit.'

Sebastian took the tray and went upstairs. The fire was blazing in the grate and all the lamps were burning brightly. Outside it was beginning to snow again. The grey sky was thick with flakes and dusk was falling. 'It's going to make it very chilly standing out there in the middle of the night,' he thought to himself. Still the main thing at the moment was to learn the poem, so he curled up in front of the fire and, between mouthfuls of toast, muttered to himself, 'O Wind, Father of the Sky...'

Several rounds of toast and three cups of tea later he felt he was beginning to get the hang of it. By half-past six, when Mrs Parkin called him down to supper he was sure he knew it perfectly. He hid the piece of paper between the pages of a book and went down to the kitchen.

Supper, as usual, was a delicious affair. Thick slices of roast beef, and roast potatoes with lots of beans and onions and horse-radish sauce, followed by a hot chocolate soufflé, crisp on the outside and creamy in the centre.

That night, as he was getting ready for bed, he looked up into the sky before drawing his curtains. The moon shone thin and silver through the still falling snow and it was almost new. 'The snow should be quite deep by the morning,' he thought to himself, 'and there will be a new moon this week.' He climbed into bed and fell straight to sleep.

The next morning he woke early. Looking out of the window, he saw that the wind had piled the snow in deep drifts against the houses, and the trees were covered with glittering crystals. Along the street the horses hooves had left round, black smudges between the tracks made by the early morning carriages. It looked very white and deep and beautiful, and the air was sharp and tingling. He longed to go out and walk in it, and hear the snow crunch beneath his feet, but first there was breakfast to be eaten and the morning's lessons to be sat through.

Mr Drycrust was in a good mood that morning, however. There is something about the first fall of deep snow which makes everyone, even the dullest of grown-ups, suddenly feel light-hearted and happy. Instead of Latin, they read a book together called *Tom Brown's Schooldays* and the hours fled past without Sebastian looking even once at the clock. Just as Mr Drycrust was leaving, Sebastian asked him if he knew when the next new moon was due. His tutor was pleased that Sebastian should show an interest in what happened to be his favourite hobby, the study of stars and planets, and he thought it a perfectly natural question. He took a little book from his pocket and

49

thumbed through the pages until he came to the one which dealt with the phases of the moon.

'Here we are, my boy,' he said in his slow, papery voice, 'the next new moon is on the fourth of December, that is, in three days time.'

'Thank you very much,' said Sebastian politely and showed him to the door. Mr Drycrust set off, looking much less huddled than usual, and he even turned round to give Sebastian a wave.

There was just enough time before lunch to go up to the attic and talk to Melissa for a while, so he quickly tidied up his lesson books and, having made sure that the coast was clear, slipped upstairs. The Mirror began to change the moment he entered the room and soon Melissa appeared, smiling and looking much happier than before. In fact the new sparkle in her eyes and the pink in her pale cheeks made her look very pretty indeed, but Sebastian didn't seem to notice.

'Hallo,' she said at once. 'I've had such fun today. It's been snowing here and Mantari and I have been playing in it. He gets so excited and chases round and round. I laughed so much it almost hurt.'

And she laughed again, and this time Sebastian couldn't fail to notice how pretty she was.

'It's been snowing here too,' he said, 'I shall go for a long walk this afternoon. I've already learnt the poem by the way, and there's a new moon in three days' time.'

'Oh good,' said Melissa. 'Everything seems to be happening all at once. One thing I'm dying to know now, is how you found the Mirror in the beginning.'

So Sebastian told her about the Teapot winking at him, and how he had gone for a walk and had found the furniture shop and...but you already know about this, Reader, and I don't expect you want to hear it all again. When he had finished, Melissa described London as she remembered it a hundred years ago, and Sebastian told her all the new things that had been invented since then, about steam engines and gaslights and iron ships.

They talked until the Mirror faded. Sebastian promised to come up to the attic the next day to see her, and Melissa smiled and vanished. Just then Mrs Parkin rang the gong for lunch, so Sebastian went down to the dining-room, feeling very happy and contented, and secretly longing for the time to come when there would be a new moon and the adventure would begin.

That afternoon he went for a walk to the large park which you can find in the centre of London. He took the Teapot with him for it had occurred to him, over lunch, that it might be possible to find out whether or not Melissa's idea about the Silver Fish was right. He remembered reading, in one of the curious old books that had belonged to his father's family for generations, that all the rivers, streams and oceans in the world were joined together, sometimes on the surface and sometimes underground. If this were so, then the Silver Fish, drawn by the attracting power between the Objects, would come to the Teapot if he placed it by some water. It was only an idea, of course, but he felt it was worth trying everything to make sure that they hadn't made a mistake. If it didn't appear, well they would just have to conclude that the cat had eaten the fish and hope for the best!

The fresh, bright air whipped his cheeks and nibbled at his fingers, but he hardly noticed it, it was so pleasant to stride out across the snow and hear it crunch under his feet like sugar. He soon reached the park and set off across the vast carpet of unbroken snow towards the river. The trees, as he walked beneath them, shed their load of white crystals, and chunks of snow fell down his back and crept between his neck and muffler. He was soon very wet indeed but he didn't care a bit, it was much too beautiful a day to worry about a little dampness. When he reached the bank of the river he found it quite deserted except for a few ducks. The water had frozen over at the edge and the ducks weren't sure what to make of the grey, glassy stuff which was so cold under their feet. Sebastian put the Teapot on the ground at a point where the river had thawed and while he waited he watched the birds slipping and sliding on the ice. They really were funny the way they tumbled over and slid along on their tail feathers, orange feet flapping madly. Sebastian laughed and laughed to see them waddling around and sliding into each other, all squeaking at the top of their voices. From time to time he glanced down at the dark brown water lying so still by his feet. No fish came to disturb it. Well, he had done all that he could so after waiting there for about an hour and a half, he picked up the Teapot and made his way slowly home to tea.

The rest of the day was spent in reading the book he had begun that morning in his lessons, and in writing a long letter to his father. He told him about all he had been doing over the past few weeks, not of course mentioning Melissa or the adventures he had been having. He did think about her though in the days which followed and went up to the attic every afternoon to talk to her.

At last it was the night of the new moon. Sebastian went up to bed, but didn't get undressed for he was afraid he might fall asleep if he got warm and comfortable. He lay on top of his bed and muttered the poem over and over to himself. He didn't feel at all sleepy, he was much too excited and perhaps just a little nervous, as I think any of us would be, at the thought of what might happen that night. When he got tired of reciting the poem, he lit a candle and read the last few chapters of his book. The hands of the library clock, which he had smuggled up to his room that evening, crept slowly round until they pointed to a quarter to twelve.

During the days he'd spent waiting for the new moon, he had decided that the best place from which to say the poem was the roof of his house. He knew that there was a skylight in one of the attic rooms and it would probably be quite a simple job to get out on to the roof. In order to have both hands free he had found a bag which he could put the Teapot in and sling round his neck. The Teapot was standing under his bed where he had hidden it a few hours ago. He felt that he had planned things quite sensibly.

At last, his heart beating loudly with excitement, he got up and, holding his boots in his hand, opened the door of his room. All was quiet. He tip-toed in his stockinged feet along the corridor to the foot of the attic stairs. Suddenly, he heard a strange rumbling sound coming from along the passage. He stood still and listened, hoping desperately that no one was awake. Then he realized what it was. Mrs Parkin was snoring gently in her sleep. He smiled to himself in the darkness and climbed the stairs to the room where the skylight was.

It all looked quite different at night. It was difficult to make out the shape of the furniture and old toys and clothes which were stored there. Everything was grey and silver, huddled around the walls, and casting out long shadows across the floor boards. Particles of dust hung glittering in the moonlight which came through the skylight. He dragged a chair across and reached up to unfasten the skylight. It opened quite easily, but with a harsh grating noise, so Sebastian had to go slowly for fear of waking someone. At last it was wide open and, as he poked his head through, the night air hit him with full force. It was bitterly cold and the wind at that height was strong and icy. Clouds rushed dark and heavy across the wide black sky and he could hear the sound of trees moaning and shaking as the gale tore between their branches. The moon was a thin white curve, hidden most of the time by the racing clouds, but breaking through from time to time to send its pale rays down on to the glistening rooftops. He hoisted himself up and climbed out on to the roof, buffeted by the wind and slipping on the thick, smooth snow. He got to his feet, wobbling dangerously, and made his way among the ridges, the Teapot banging against him, towards the chimney-stack. He grabbed hold of this with relief for the wind was catching his hair and whipping it against his face and into his eyes, making it difficult to see. Before him stretched a jumble of white rooftops, and here and there the spire of a church rose up and pointed its grey turret to the sky. A bell tolled midnight, its clanging

almost drowned by the roar of the wind which wildly
fought the trees and buildings. Sebastian was beginning to
feel chilled to the bone, and so, holding on tightly and
shutting his eyes, he shouted the poem as loudly as he
could, above the gale. Then he opened his eyes and looked
around, his heart thumping so fast that it hurt. It seemed
at first as if nothing had happened. The wind howled as
loudly as ever and Sebastian felt ready to die from

disappointment and the cold. Then he saw that the sky was changing above his head. The clouds were rushing towards each other and swirling into an enormous circle which spread across the sky. And then Sebastian realized that it was a great face looking down at him, so vast that he had to twist his head back to see it. In the centre were two dark patches which made the eyes and in the middle of each shone two bright stars. Sebastian was so awed and terrified that he couldn't think what to do. He just stood there, clinging on to the chimney-stack for dear life and staring up into the huge face above him. Then he saw a gap appear in the face where the mouth was and he heard a voice which was very loud and yet was like a whisper, the sound of a thousand trees rustling in a great forest.

'Welcome, Summoner,' it said, 'you have come to drive out evil and your heart is good. I know you seek the Emerald of the Enchanter and I shall help you. Have no fear. Close your eyes, and do not open them until I tell you.'

Sebastian did as he was told, feeling afraid, and yet full of excitement and a curious kind of joy.

'Now,' said the voice, 'hold out your hands towards me.'

Sebastian let go of the chimney-stack and lifted his arms above his head. At once he felt himself drawn up into the sky and thrown on to the breath of the Wind. Faster and faster he whirled and the roar of the Wind in his ears was deafening. But he wasn't cold. A delicious warmth crept up from his toes and spread through his whole body, and as he was rushed, twisting and turning, through the sky, he felt wildly happy and filled with a wonderful peace and feeling of utter contentment. He forgot everything, who he was, where he came from, where he was going, he even forgot about Melissa. He wanted only to go on spinning among the stars for ever and ever and never come to rest. But after what seemed like a thousand years and yet could have been only a few seconds, the voice of the Wind whispered to him through his dreams.

'Now, gentle Summoner, open your eyes and behold.'

And when Sebastian opened them, he saw that he was rushing towards a great mountain. The ground was spread far below him and it was bright daylight, so he could see the tops of tiny trees bending in the blast of the Wind. The mountain grew larger at every moment and Sebastian began to wonder if he would be dashed to pieces against it. It was sheer rock with no trees to soften its spiked pinnacles, and he began to feel alarmed. Then he saw that a short way down from the top of the mountain was a gaping black hole and he seemed to be going straight towards it. Sure enough, in another few seconds he was blown quickly but gently right into the mouth of a very large cave. He landed with a thud.

'Good luck,' said the whispering voice. There was a loud rushing sound and then silence. Feeling dazed and giddy, Sebastian looked around him. The roof of the cave was very high, it came to a pointed arch in the centre and the whole ceiling had been intricately carved. It's beauty was exquisite and Sebastian at once realized that no ordinary person lived here, for it was certainly no ordinary craftsman who had wrought such perfection. The floor of the cave was perfectly smooth and covered with a thin layer of fine silvery sand, which sparkled here and there in the light. There were four small caves leading off the main one and when Sebastian went over to have a closer look he found that in each one there was a sort of bed made of woven grasses. They looked terribly comfortable and reminded him that he was missing a night's sleep. It would be silly to start out on an adventure feeling exhausted and it didn't seem as if the owner of the cave was going to appear yet, so there couldn't be any harm in just resting for a little as long as he didn't go to sleep. He chose the

57

cave nearest the mouth and settled down on the strange mattress. 'Gosh, this is comfortable,' he said to himself, 'I wonder who...' and immediately fell fast asleep.

He was woken by a dry scraping sound close to his ear, and by something touching his face. He sat up with a start and clutched at the thing which had fallen on to him. It was a leaf, curled up at the edges and a lovely orange-gold colour. Sebastian looked at it, and listened carefully. Then he heard the scraping sound again, coming from the main cave. It was accompanied by a low muttering. Sebastian got up quietly and peered round the rock in the direction of the noise. What he saw gave him such a shock that he almost cried out in surprise. A tall skinny man was standing at the entrance of the cave with his back to Sebastian. He was looking up into the sky and either muttering or humming a little tune to himself. But what was most extraordinary was the way he was dressed. He was clad from head to foot in leaves. Brown leaves, red leaves, orange leaves and yellow leaves, some wrapped tightly round his body and some dripping from his elbows and hanging round his head. Suddenly he turned round and a shower of leaves fell to the ground.

'Bother,' said this extraordinary person and he bent down, scraped the leaves in a heap and pushed them out of the cave into the valley, below. Then he saw Sebastian, who was standing staring at him with his mouth open.

'Hallo,' said the leafy man, 'did I wake you up? I'm very sorry. It's difficult not to be noisy with all these leaves rustling about.'

Sebastian continued to stare and say nothing. He was looking at the man's eyes, which were round and brown and shiny and looked very much like two chestnuts.

'I say,' said the man, 'you do understand English, don't you? Surely those are English clothes you're wearing?'

58

Sebastian found his tongue. 'Yes, they are. I'm sorry to stare, I didn't mean to be rude. I was just rather astonished by your—by your,' Sebastian had been going to say 'appearance' but then thought that it might offend him, so his voice trailed away while he tried to think of a better way of putting it.

The leafy man laughed, and another shower of leaves fell to the ground. 'I understand completely,' he said, 'I must look very odd indeed to you. Actually I'm just as surprised to see you here, as you are to see me. I tell you what. Let's just tidy up these leaves before Ver gets back, she gets so cross you know, if I leave my leaves about, and then we can get to know each other.' Then he knelt down with a lot of rustling, losing a few more leaves in the process, and began to collect them all together, talking all the while. 'It's a very good thing that you're English,' he said, 'as naturally I've just been over there and the language is quite fresh in my mind. By the summer I get quite rusty again.'

'When exactly were you there, then?' asked Sebastian, thinking that he must have looked even more extraordinary there, than he did here.

'Why in the autumn, of course,' said his companion with a laugh. 'When else? I love England, I must say. I feel quite envious of Hiems at the moment.'

'Hiems?' said Sebastian. 'Isn't that the Latin word for "Winter"?'

The leafy man stopped picking up the leaves and looked at Sebastian in surprise. 'Oh dear,' he said, 'how rude of me not to introduce myself. I just thought you'd know where you were, or else you wouldn't be here. This is where the Seasons live, of course. I'm Autumnus, which means "Autumn" in your language of course, and then there's Hiems which, as you so rightly guessed, means "Winter" and of course Ver and Aestas, "Spring" and "Summer" to you. Well, this is quite a mystery. I always try never to be surprised by anything, but this is very odd indeed. Suppose you tell me how you got here, and how we can help you?'

And so saying, he sat down on the sandy floor and patted the patch of ground beside him. Sebastian sat down, feeling fascinated and confused. It was certainly an occasion to remember, sitting down with Autumn and talking like old friends!

'Have something to eat,' said Autumnus, and suddenly produced a large red apple from the leaves about his person. Sebastian took it and bit off a large chunk. It was by far the best he had ever eaten, hard and juicy and very sweet. Autumnus had one too, and for a moment they were silent except for loud munching noises. Then Autumnus threw his core out of the cave and Sebastian when he had finished his, did the same. A few seconds later, there was a little scream and someone was standing in the entrance, rubbing her cheek and looking very angry. She was tall and thin like Autumnus, and quite as extra-ordinary-looking but in a different way. Her skin seemed to be made of petals which clung together to form a delicate cobwebby pattern. From her head drooped thousands of soft, curling feathers which fluttered and floated around her. They were all different colours, pale yellow, gold, soft pink, turquoise and mauve. Her dress hung down to her feet and trailed out behind her. It was made just of flowers, crocuses, snowdrops, daffodils, primroses, oh, all the spring flowers you can think of. It was a beautiful sight, and the scent of the flowers filled the cave and made Sebastian's nose tingle. However, the expression on her face was rather worrying.

'I suppose this must be Spring, or Ver rather?' he whispered to Autumnus.

Ver, as of course it was, heard Sebastian whispering, and

stalked over to him. She looked him up and down and then said something to Autumnus which Sebastian didn't understand, but which sounded rather cross.

'Now, Ver,' said Autumnus, 'don't be silly. This is our guest and he didn't mean to hit you with the apple core. It was an accident. He's from England, and you know how charming the English are. Let me introduce you. Ver, this is—come to think of it, I don't know your name yet.'

Sebastian stood up and gave a little bow. 'My name is Sebastian,' he said, 'I'm so sorry to have hurt you. I really didn't mean to, and I'm very, very pleased to meet you.'

Ver looked rather less cross at this. She said that it was all right, she forgave him and she quite understood Sebastian being pleased to meet her. Sebastian thought this sounded rather conceited, but Autumnus told him in a whisper that Ver was very vain and not to mind her. She was a good sort really, it was just that she was young.

'What are you two whispering about?' asked Ver.

'We were just talking about you,' said Autumnus. Ver patted her feathers and gave a little flounce and coy look. She never doubted that they were admiring her.

'Well,' she said, 'what I'd like to know, is what you're doing here.' She said it kindly though and seemed to be pleased that Sebastian was there, now that she'd got used to the idea.

'I'd like to know that too,' said Autumnus, 'but I think we ought to wait for Hiems and Aestas before Sebastian begins. That way he will only have to tell his story once.'

'That seems sensible,' agreed Ver. 'I'll tidy up while we're waiting. I expect your leaves are everywhere again.'

'Actually, I've cleared them up,' said Autumnus, 'but you've dropped some feathers and petals over there.'

Ver looked annoyed for a moment and then she laughed. 'All right, Autumnus. I'm sorry to be bad-tempered, it's just that I've been working so hard today. I shall have to speak to Hiems about freezing the soil too much. It's been exhausting trying to make things grow. Have an egg, Sebastian,' and she held out a small bluey-green egg which she had found among her feathers.

He took it. It was smooth and cool in his hand. He didn't really know what to do with it for he didn't like eggs raw, but he also didn't want to hurt her feelings. Autumnus understood however.

'Humans don't eat raw eggs, Ver,' he told her, 'let's wait for Aestas and she can cook it for our friend.'

Ver seemed amused rather than hurt at the idea, and Sebastian breathed a quiet sigh of relief.

'Let's entertain our guest with a few songs,' suggested Autumnus.

So he and Ver sang together in a strange language which Sebastian didn't understand, but the tune was so delightful and their voices blended together so well, that Sebastian thought it was the loveliest sound he had ever heard.

Suddenly a blast of freezing air swept through the cave and there, towering in the entrance, so magnificent that Sebastian gasped aloud, was Hiems or, as we call him, Winter. He was at least a foot taller than Ver and Autumnus and dressed in a sort of tunic of thick white fur trimmed with diamonds. His skin was white also, it shimmered as he moved and shot out silver sparks all around him. Around his neck, wrists and ankles hung spikes of ice and on his head was a tall crown of icicles, each point needle-sharp. The most marvellous and terrifying thing about him though, were his eyes. They were a deep turquoise blue and they seemed to pierce straight through anything he bent his gaze upon. As he looked at Sebastian he seemed to be searching into his heart, and Sebastian felt terribly uncomfortable and rather small.

'Welcome, Englishman,' he said at last, and his voice

was deep and powerful and calm. Sebastian stood up and tried not to look nervous. Autumnus made the introductions. Hiems smiled at Sebastian and at once he stopped feeling afraid, and felt only respect and awe. He noticed that Hiems' teeth were made of blocks of ice, clear and sharply pointed.

'I have heard,' said the God of Winter, 'that you are seeking the Emerald of the Enchanter.'

'Yes, I am,' answered Sebastian, wondering how on earth he knew.

Hiems understood what he was thinking. 'The Wind told me as we strolled together across the continents.' Sebastian suddenly had the feeling that everything in the world was much larger and more mysterious than he had ever dreamed it could be.

'Yes, you are right,' said Hiems suddenly and Sebastian realized that he had read his thoughts. 'However,' continued this great prince, 'before we discuss your problem, we must wait for Aestas who, as usual, is late. Let us talk of the things we three have seen today, which I think Sebastian will find interesting.'

And indeed it was. He listened, fascinated, while they described to him the countries and the worlds they had visited and he soon forgot about the unknown dangers which lay ahead. Hiems didn't say as much as the others as he had spent a lot of time in England of course, but Autumnus was very amusing, and Ver was interesting as well, although she tended to boast rather.

At last Aestas arrived. She came tumbling into the cave, laughing happily to herself. When she had managed to untangle herself from the folds of her long green robe, Sebastian found himself looking up into a bright, smiling face which was a beautiful soft green. Her eyes were amber-coloured and glowed like twin suns, and her hair was a mass of daisies which swept down her back almost to the floor in a sheet of white petals speckled with yellow pollen. Her green robe swirled around her constantly and disappeared into a floating mist around her feet. Sebastian suddenly felt very happy too, and then, for no reason at all he began to laugh. The others joined in too, and for several minutes they all laughed together in the greatest possible merriment. When they had calmed down at last, Autumnus explained to Sebastian that Aestas always had this effect on people and it was something to do with the sun. Hadn't he noticed how, on the first day of proper sunshine each year, everyone was good-humoured and happy. Now that Sebastian thought about it he realized that this was indeed true.

At this point, Hiems suggested that they should all have something to eat while Sebastian told them why he was looking for the Emerald.

They dined on honey and nuts and fruit, and eggs which Aestas obligingly held in her hands until they were cooked. Ver crushed some small flowers and collected the juice in a strange waxy flower, shaped rather like an egg-cup. This made a refreshing drink. Between mouthfuls, Sebastian told them the whole story, from the moment that the Teapot had winked at him right up to the time when he had found himself in the Cave of the Four Seasons. They were good listeners and didn't interrupt at all (except for Ver who wanted to know if Melissa was very pretty, but was silenced by a glance from Hiems). When Sebastian had finished, they all said how sorry they were for poor Melissa and that they would do everything in their power to help her. Then Hiems assumed authority.

'I presume that the Wind sent you to us because he thought we would probably have seen the Emerald on our travels. Each of us visits every inch of every world once a year. Let's see if any of us can remember where it is.'

And they all sat back and shut their eyes. Their faces, one

64

leafy, one green, one flowery and one snow-white were so tranquil and removed, that Sebastian began to wonder if they had all fallen asleep. He didn't know whether he should wake them or if that would be impolite. Just as he decided that it would be better to let them wake of their own accord, Aestas suddenly shouted, 'I've got it!' and at once they were all alert and listening. Aestas looked grave which was very rare for her.

'Oh dear, this is going to be difficult indeed,' she said. 'Let me tell you the whole story. One day, several hundred years ago, I was passing by the Grey Forest which lies in the Silent Valley, and I was thinking how dreadful the Forest looked. So gloomy and ugly and dark. I decided to try a little sunlight to see if that would make it any less horrible. I sent several beams between the branches and along the ground, but as soon as my rays met the trees they turned quite grey. I felt even more depressed then, and decided to try from above, so I called over a small breeze which happened to come by at that moment. It carried me up over the tree-tops and I sent a shaft of sunlight down into the heart of the Forest. It passed through the branches and hit the ground. As before, the beam turned grey as soon as it entered the Forest, but where it met the earth, a pure, green light shone up from the undergrowth. At my command the breeze carried me lower over the trees and I saw that the glow came from a huge stone, an emerald, the largest I had ever seen. It lay there, hidden from man's eye, in the depths of the Forest which we are forbidden to enter. By this time I was behind in my day's work and I was also getting rather blown about, so I decided to leave the Valley and come back another day. Well, the days passed into weeks, and the months into years, and gradually I forgot all about it. It was, however, no ordinary stone which could resist the power of the Grey Forest and regain its colour in my shaft of light.'

They looked at one another in dismay. 'I think this must be the stone you are looking for, Sebastian,' said Hiems at last, 'I know of no other emerald which possesses a magic power. What do you others say.'

Autumnus and Ver shook their heads gloomily. 'No, said the former, 'I think this is the one all right. The Enchanter couldn't have chosen a better place to hide it that's for certain.'

At this point Sebastian begged them to tell him about the Grey Forest and why they were so dismayed that the Emerald was there.

'Well,' said Hiems, 'the first disadvantage is that we four are forbidden to enter the Forest in any circumstances whatever, by Time, who is our master. Were we our own rulers, we would gladly enter the Forest with you, but we must answer to Time, and that has been laid down since the creation of the first living thing. However each of us may help you in our own way, through our power over all growing things. You may call on each of us just once, and no more, and you yourself must judge the best time to do it, for I cannot foretell exactly what danger you may face. I can, however, warn you of the power which the Forest has. The trees are evil and they have the power of everlasting sleep. They remove your strength to resist this enchantment by their ability to make man's thought sinful. Once wickedness has entered your heart, they have you in their grasp. Now that you know this, it may be possible for you to pass through the Forest unharmed, but only if you keep it firmly in your mind that you must not listen to the trees. Do you feel you are strong enough for this?'

Sebastian sat silent for a moment. His heart beat heavily and he felt afraid. But could he just give up here and leave Melissa imprisoned in the Treasure House forever He would never be able to forgive himself for his cowardice

if he did. No, he would have to find courage from somewhere and face the dangers that lay ahead, no matter how
great.

'Well done,' said Hiems suddenly, 'your fear does you no
discredit. Only a fool could think lightly of the matter and
the decision you have taken is a brave one.'

Sebastian had forgotten that Hiems had the power to
read his thoughts, and for a moment he felt ashamed of
being afraid, but the smile which Hiems gave him was one
of approval and not contempt, so he felt better about it.

'Now,' said Hiems, 'I think we should all get some sleep.
Tomorrow we shall escort you to the Forest. I would offer
to share my bed, Sebastian, but I think you would find it
rather cold.'

'There's plenty of room with me,' said Autumnus, and
Sebastian gratefully accepted his offer. One thing was
worrying him though.

'It will be nearly morning at home, now,' he said, 'I
don't want to make a fuss, but won't they be awfully
worried when they find me gone?'

'Did I not tell you that we serve under Time?' said
Hiems. 'While you are under our protection you are also
under his, therefore. Do not be worried. You will see that it
will be all right. You have already learnt, through your
visit to the Treasure House, that Time is not the same in
all worlds. Now, let us rest, and save our energies for the
morrow.'

So Sebastian curled up beside Autumnus and very soon
fell asleep.

While Sebastian slept in the Cave of the Seasons, Melissa was sitting in the gold-and-silver room of the Treasure House, staring out through the windows into the garden below, and wondering what was happening to Sebastian. Mantari lay curled into a ball on her knee and was sleeping peacefully, his fine orange ears twitching now and then as he dreamed.

Suddenly, with a low growl, he sat up, and in a moment was wide awake. He shook himself, rubbed his furry cheek against Melissa's hand, and then sprang over to the door, where he turned round and held Melissa in a long steady gaze.

'What on earth's the matter?' said Melissa, 'do you want to go out?'

Mantari miaowed, and stalked up and down beside the door. Melissa got up and opened it for him and at once the cat fled through, shot down the corridor, and whisked out of sight down the stairs.

'That's strange,' thought Melissa to herself. 'I wonder what's upset him?'

And then in a flash she knew, for a second later, just a few feet from where she was standing, a small puff of green smoke rose up from the floor, and then, with a clap of thunder which shook the Treasure House from end to end, the Enchanter towered before her. This had happened

nearly a hundred times before, but Melissa still couldn't help feeling nervous whenever it did.

The Enchanter looked at her with his cruel, black eyes and then smiled, and it was a smile which made Melissa turn cold and the blood drain from her face, so full of malice and evil was it.

69

'You have, I trust, spent the year pleasantly,' said the Enchanter, with a sneer. 'Not too lonely, I hope?' and he laughed nastily.

'You know the answer to that,' said Melissa, with as much dignity as she could find. The Enchanter laughed again, and then he stopped and began to look at her closely. A furrow appeared on his forehead, and a gleam of suspicion grew in place of the mocking evil in his eyes.

'There are laughter lines around your mouth,' he said slowly, 'and your eyes are clear and bright. No tear has crept from under those lids recently. So something has made you happier, has it? I should like to know precisely what that something is.' And he leaned towards her threateningly.

'I would have thought,' said Melissa coldly, trying hard to keep the panic out of her voice, 'that with all your power, you would be clever enough to realize that there is nothing that can help me now, other than my own wish to spend the endless years in as much contentment as possible. I may be only a child but I have had many years to practise the art of making the best of things, and in that, at least, there is nothing you can do to stop me.'

The Enchanter looked angry for a moment and then his mouth twisted into a smile. 'You are quite right. There is nothing that can help you now. Furthermore, there is no reason why I should wish your misery to be as great as possible. It was your guardian and not you, yourself, who made the promise and tricked me, after all. I am not a cruel man.' But the laughter which followed belied his words and Melissa knew that she was going to have to be very careful indeed not to spoil everything.

Soon the Enchanter left to look at his treasures, which were stored behind all the locked doors of the Treasure House and she was left alone again.

'Good luck, Sebastian,' she whispered to herself and the

rest of the day, until the Enchanter went back to his castle, was spent in an agony of suspense which didn't really leave her until the night fell and Mantari returned.

Sebastian woke up feeling rather cold, and found Hiems standing over him, holding something towards him which steamed and smoked. It was a large sea-shell, filled with a warm fragrant liquid. Hiems explained that Ver had made him a sort of wine-cup and Aestas had heated it for him, in case he found the cave rather chilly. Sebastian drank it quickly. It tasted delicious, and it must have gone to his head, for he began to feel very gay and happy and quite ready for anything. Everyone else was wide awake, and Ver had apparently already been out, catching up on the work she hadn't finished the day before. They ate a small breakfast together of much the same things they had eaten a few hours before. Sebastian began to feel that Mrs Parkin's cooking would be very welcome if and when, he got back, but of course he didn't say so. Then, to his horror, he saw that Hiems was watching him closely and there was a twinkle in those sharp blue eyes.

'Golly, how awful,' thought Sebastian, 'he read my thoughts again. He must think I'm very ungrateful.'

'Not at all,' said Hiems, 'we come from different races, ages and worlds. If food were the only difference between us, it would make existence a very dull thing, don't you think?'

Sebastian was very flattered to have his opinion asked by the great god Winter and was too shy to do more than nod, but he felt Hiems' kindness towards him and was glad of it.

When they had finished, Ver rushed round tidying up the Cave and then they were ready to go. Sebastian looked down into the valley below and felt a little uneasy. He didn't like heights very much, and to climb down the sheer rock face seemed almost impossible. Then Hiems took him firmly by one hand and Autumnus by the other, and all five of them leapt out into the sky in a shower of leaves and feathers.

Sebastian found that they were all running at a tremendous speed and slowly descending across the valley. Aestas was a little ahead of them, her green robe billowing round her and disappearing into wisps around her feet. Sebastian saw that the soles of her feet were green too. It was a strange feeling, running through the air, and, looking at the enormous drop below him, he felt very glad of the strong grasp on either side. They passed through a gap in the mountains ahead of them and went still lower, until they were only a few feet from the ground. Sebastian felt much better about this, and began to enjoy himself. They passed over rocky country, where crags of red stone jutted up from the white sand and scratched the sky. Then they came to greener lands where yellow stalks of wheat bent their heads and whispered gently to each other as they passed. The journey seemed to be endless and after an hour or so Sebastian was quite exhausted. It was much easier to run through the air than on the ground, and Hiems and Autumnus were probably doing most of the work, but all the same Sebastian's legs were beginning to ache unbearably. At last they came into a valley, which looked quite different from the others they had passed through. It was grim and silent. Sebastian noticed that the air was thicker and much harder to run through. He didn't need to be told that this was the Silent Valley. They came gently down to the ground and Sebastian found that he had to sit down, his legs were too tired to support him. There in front of them, rose a tall, dark forest. It spread as far as the eye could see, and heavy branches overhung the edges and cast them into deep shade. Sebastian didn't like the look of it all. The others stood and stared around them.

'Well, Sebastian,' said Hiems at last, 'this is the Grey Forest and somewhere in the middle of that is your Emerald. Do you feel rested now?'

Sebastian very much wanted to wait a little longer but he knew that it was because he was afraid, and not because he was tired. The effects of the wine-cup had worn off now and he felt cold and lonely.

'Yes, I think I'll go now,' he said, hoping that the others didn't know how frightened he was.

'Right then. Remember that you may ask each of us for help just once, and that you must not listen to the trees. We shall wait for you here. Keep a brave heart and may luck go with you.'

Sebastian set off to walk the distance between him and the Forest's edge. Hiems' warning was ringing in his ears. The air became heavier and heavier, the nearer he got to the trees.

'This is the worst thing I've had to face so far,' he thought to himself. 'Magic can be quite unpleasant at times I must say. I almost wish that I'd never got involved in this.' But this was a cowardly thought and he dismissed it from his mind. It wasn't going to help at this stage to think that sort of thing. He was nearly at the edge of the Forest by now, and he agreed with Aestas that it was ugly. The trunks of the trees were a horrible dull grey and so were the leaves and the bushes and the ground beneath them. It didn't smell like an ordinary forest either, no leafy scents or whiffs of pine and damp bracken. It smelt as musty as a tomb and slightly sickly. He turned back to look at the others. They were all sitting down and had their faces turned towards him. Hiems lifted his hand in a salute. Sebastian waved back with a casualness he didn't feel, and then he turned round and stepped into the Forest.

It was deathly quiet but for the snapping of twigs and undergrowth beneath his feet. Grey brambles kept catching on his clothes and scratching his legs. As he bent down to untangle himself from the sharp spikes which clutched at his ankles, he saw that his hands and legs were quite grey. In fact his whole body had turned the colour of the trees and bushes. The thought made Sebastian shiver. The musty smell began to make him feel rather dizzy. It seemed to press down on him and he felt as if something were tugging him back, each time he took a step forward. The trees rose up beside him tall, dark and unmoving. Their trunks were wrinkled with age and the leaves hung limp like dead hands. Now and then they brushed against his face, and where they had touched him, his skin felt damp and sticky. He made his way in the direction of the heart of the Forest, growing more tired at every step. He had come some way from the edge of the Forest now, and here the trees grew closer together and it was very dark indeed.

At last he felt he must have a rest so he sat down carefully on a broken branch which lay across the grey earth. He looked at his hands. They had blood on them where the brambles had torn them, and it was black. They stung a little, and the branch he was sitting on poked him in the back. 'Gosh, this is uncomfortable,' he thought to himself,

'I never imagined that a place could be so horrible. And all this for a girl, too. If I wasn't a pretty nice person, I'd leave her there and save myself. I could be sitting in front of the fire, reading a good book, if it wasn't for her. Anyway, how do I know I'll get out of here after all this? She's better off there than I'd be if I got enchanted and had to sleep here forever.' And just as he thought this he remembered Hiems' warning. He suddenly realized it wasn't him thinking this at all. There was a quiet little voice coming from the tree behind him, saying all these dreadful cowardly things. He could hear it now, whispering to him, trying to persuade him that he was far too brave and clever to risk his life for a girl.

'No, no, no!' shouted Sebastian. 'I'm not brave and clever at all. I won't listen to you. You're evil, and I won't let you make me cruel!'

And he jumped up and started to run. As he fought his way through the undergrowth, he could hear the voices of the trees telling him not to be so stupid, what would his father think if his brave, clever, handsome son vanished forever. 'My father would hate me to be a coward,' said Sebastian to himself over and over again, and he refused to listen to the voices. 'I don't believe you,' he shouted from time to time, and thrust the branches away from his face. 'It's no use talking to me. You won't make me listen.' And slowly the voices died away and the Forest was quiet again. He came to a standstill, panting heavily, and the blood pounding in his ears. He had lost all sense of direction now, and had no idea which way the centre of the Forest lay. He looked around him carefully, determined to keep calm. Then he saw, in the shadows under a great spreading branch, a man lying on the ground. Sebastian's heart leapt to his mouth and almost stopped beating. He tip-toed forward to have a closer look. It was a very old man. His grey beard was tangled around his feet and his clothes were

75

worn to shreds. He was lying crumpled on his side, sleeping
heavily and quite, quite still. His body cast a dark grey
shadow on the ground.

Sebastian looked at him, and a great sadness overcame
him. He walked away slowly, and determined to remember
the scene as a warning, should the trees try to talk to him
again. He decided that his best plan was to keep walking
straight ahead and he remembered with a twinge of fear
the stories he'd heard about people getting lost in forests,
and walking round in circles. He struggled on, thinking

about the man he had found and wondering if there was anything which could help him. He realized now how easy it was to be tricked by those cunning trees, and his heart was full of pity for their victim. Then he noticed that the ground under his feet was getting soggy and it seemed to cling to his boots with a sucking noise. He thought that he must be approaching some sort of swamp, which alarmed him very much, and he was extremely careful about where he put his feet. Sure enough, he soon found that he was walking along a narrow path, and on either side of him lurked evil-smelling pools. The air was so sickly now and so thick with the steam which rose from the dark water, that he began to feel quite ill. The path got more and more narrow. In some places it was no more than a few inches wide. It seemed to be getting darker too. The trees bent over him and their leaves tangled together so that very little light came through. He looked up and watched the branches slowly moving over him and then suddenly, with a tightening feeling around his heart, he realized that they were closing together deliberately, to prevent him from seeing his way. Now, with a great rustling sound, the branches above him embraced each other. It was pitch black. Sebastian stood still, very frightened now, and not daring to take another step in case he slipped into the swamp. He hugged himself tightly, and kept telling himself that if he didn't move he would be all right. He could hear the faint lapping of the water in the darkness. It seemed to beckon to him to end this misery and fear, and find relief in its soothing arms. He opened his mouth and his voice came out in a whisper which trembled through the steaming blackness. 'Autumnus, help me now.' The trees overhead began to stir and then he felt things brushing against him, and heard them falling into the water with a soft plop! Gradually it began to get lighter and, through the gloom, Sebastian saw that the leaves above him were drifting slowly round and down, and soon the branches showed sharp and bare in the pale grey light which fell across the steaming pools. 'Thank you, Autumnus,' murmured Sebastian, with heart-felt relief, and he picked his way along the path as quickly as possible until he reached dry ground again. There he paused to quieten his thumping heart and gather all his energy and courage to go on. He tried to work out how far he had come, and supposed that by now he must be somewhere near the middle of the Forest, so he called out, this time in a much louder voice, 'Aestas, help me now.' And there, in the distance, a thin shaft of grey light came through the trees and where it reached the ground he could see something green and glowing. It was so wonderful to see a colour which was rich and pure after all the greyness that Sebastian felt suddenly much less tired and frightened. He set off towards the glowing light, pushing his way through the undergrowth, and picturing the joy on Melissa's face when he showed her the Emerald at last. But when he got to the place where the light was coming from, his heart sank. The biggest emerald you can imagine, was lying embedded in moss on a jagged rock, and it was surrounded on all sides by water, which bubbled and churned with an angry, hissing noise. It was too wide to jump, and anyway if he could have reached the middle, the rock looked so steep and slippery that he would probably just slide off into the water. The Emerald shone, pure and radiant and impossible to reach. Sebastian felt like bursting into tears. A little voice began to whisper to him. 'You see, it really was a waste of time, wasn't it? Isn't it annoying that you've come all this way, to be cheated at the last moment. It really doesn't pay to help people, does it?' Sebastian thought of the man lying somewhere in this horrible Forest, doomed to sleep forever, and he shut his ears to the persistent little voice.

'Hiems,' he called loudly, 'help me now.'

There was a cracking noise, and something seemed to be happening to the churning water. Round the edges it grew flat and shiny and very pale, and the bubbling gradually grew still. It was ice, creeping over the surface, and spreading its cold fingers right out to the edge of the rock. Sebastian put one foot on it. It was hard and solid. Cautiously he stepped forward on to the frozen surface. It showed no sign of giving way beneath his weight. He made his way slowly, and at last he reached out and picked the Emerald from its bed of moss. It glowed for a moment and then turned grey, for it was no longer under Aestas' beam of sunlight. Sebastian didn't mind though. It felt warm and reassuring in his hand, and he made his way back over the ice in a glow of joy and triumph.

'I know I couldn't have done it without the others, though,' he said aloud to the trees, 'so don't think you can try and make me proud about it, so there!'

The trees were silent. He tried to find his way back the same way he had come, but after a while he realized that he had taken a wrong turning somewhere. He kept on going, his head aching from the heavy air which pressed down on him. He began to feel very tired again. Then to his dismay he saw that he was approaching the very rock on which he had found the Emerald. The ice had gone now, and the water hissed and spat angrily at him. 'I must have done a complete circle,' he thought to himself, 'this is hopeless. I might be wandering around for days, and the trees are bound to get me sooner or later. I shall be too exhausted to resist them. So he lifted his head and called, 'Ver, help me now.'

There was a twittering sound and there, a few yards away, perched on a twig with his head on one side, was a tiny greyish-yellow bird. It hopped up and down and then flew into the air and beat its pale wings around Sebastian's head.

'Why, hallo,' said Sebastian, 'have you come to show me the way?'

The little bird chirped and fluttered and then flew off in front of him. Sebastian followed. The bird went quite slowly and now and then it settled on to a branch to wait for him. It looked very beautiful in the gloom of the Forest, and even among all the twisting branches which stretched down over him, Sebastian never lost sight of the little yellow light, hopping and fluttering before him. He was very thankful that they went a different way from the one he had come by, and there were no swamps or brambles to be seen. It was still a long way though, and all the hours he had spent breathing the musty air made his head reel and his limbs feel heavy. It was all he could do to keep his eyes on the beating wings ahead, and stumble on. It became like a dream, and just as he was thinking that he would never wake up from it, and would go stumbling on forever, he saw that the trees were growing thinner and there was light ahead. A moment later, and he was out of the Forest and blinking in the light of day, and there in the distance, calling and waving, were Hiems, Aestas, Ver and dear old, leafy Autumnus. He looked at the Emerald in his hand. It was a pure, vivid green, and he saw with happiness that his hand was back to its normal colour again. The tiny bird sang and chirruped above him and its feathers were a bright, glowing gold. His heart almost bursting with joy, Sebastian gathered together all the strength he had left, and ran over to where the others were waiting for him, the bird swooping and singing in his wake.

When he tried to think, in later years, what they had said to him and he had said to them on that happy meeting, it was difficult to remember anything but Hiems' proudly smiling face, and how they had all roared with laughter, with Aestas falling over her robe and laughing the loudest of them all. They ended up in a great heap of leaves, feathers and flowers, Aestas' glowing eyes shining on Autumnus' chestnut ones and spreading light all over the Silent Valley, which seemed so much less dismal than before.

When they had recovered, and Sebastian had thanked them all for their help, and been hugged hotly by Aestas, they held hands and glided into the air and out of the Valley. Ver carried the Emerald and it glittered and glowed before them. The journey back to the Cave seemed much shorter now that they were all so happy, and in no time at all they were running and floating up the sheer mountain-side to the Cave of the Seasons. They swept in and sank down on to the shimmering, silvery floor.

'Now,' said Aestas, 'the next thing is to refresh ourselves with some of your very good wine-cup, Ver, if you would be so kind.' So Ver plucked some flowers from her robe and crushed them over the shells which Autumnus fetched from the back of the cave. The juices trickled out, purple and rich, and then Aestas held each shell in her hands until the liquid began to froth and bubble. Sebastian drank his quickly and soon felt warm and very happy. It seemed to have the same effect on the others, too. Hiems' turquoise eyes positively twinkled, and thousands of silver sparks shot away from him and lay sizzling on the sand until they went out. One landed on Sebastian and it felt very cold indeed, but in quite a pleasant, tingly way. He was astonished that Autumnus had any leaves left at all with all the laughing he was doing, there was a constant rustling and crackling as they fell off. But it seemed that they were replaced instantly, for he remained quite as leafy as before.

Sebastian told them about the man he had found sleeping in the Forest. They were very sad about this, and wondered if there was any way to help him.

'After all,' said Hiems, 'no human is perfect, and I expect those trees can be very convincing!'

'They certainly can,' said Sebastian, with a shudder, as he thought of what might have happened if he hadn't remembered Hiems' warning in time.

'It really isn't painful, I shouldn't think,' put in Autumnus comfortably. 'I don't suppose they feel anything at all. It's just a terrible waste of life.'

'Supposing they have nightmares though?' said Ver. Hiems frowned at her. Sebastian hadn't thought of that before, and it made him feel even more unhappy about it. He could see the man so clearly in his mind, among the shadows, and the steaming air of the Forest.

'Why don't you look in the Book of the Enchanter when you get back?' suggested Hiems, 'those sort of books usually have every sort of enchantment listed in them. I've seen one like it before, about three hundred years ago, but I should think it was less powerful. There are five of them I think.'

'That seems to be a magic number,' said Sebastian.

'It's one of them,' agreed Hiems. 'Anyway, you might find a way in your Book to help the man, that is, if you've the strength for more adventures?'

'I'll jolly well have a go anyway,' said Sebastian. 'And now I think I should go back. You probably all have a lot of work to do, and thank you so much for taking time off to help me.'

Autumnus beamed. 'I told you the English were charming and considerate didn't I?' he said, jumping up and down and covering everybody with bits and pieces of leaf. Hiems calmed him down, and they all sadly said their goodbyes.

'Just a moment,' said Sebastian, 'how do I get back, anyway?'

'The same way as you came,' said Hiems smiling at him. 'You haven't forgotten the poem have you?'

82

'No,' said Sebastian, 'but what about a new moon and everything?'

'Look behind you,' said Hiems.

Sebastian, who had been standing with his back to the entrance of the Cave, turned round. Through the entrance hung a sky the colour of a grape, blue and purple, and soft as velvet. Here and there clouds stood still and silent among a spread of silver stars. A yellow moon shone, like a shallow smile, over the valley.

'You see,' said Hiems softly, 'Time is our master and he grants us favours in the name of Good. We wish you well Sebastian, all of us including Time. Here is the Teapot. Take it, with our dearest hopes for your happiness and Melissa's. Farewell.'

Sebastian took a last glimpse of their smiling faces, and then turned to the great sky. He put the bag holding the Teapot round his neck, shut his eyes and said the poem. It echoed through the valley, and the mountains on the other side seemed to chant it after him, as if to make sure that its message was heard. There was a rushing sound, and then the clouds surged together until they had formed the huge face of the Wind.

'Well done!' came the voice which was a roar and yet a whisper. The words sung in his ears as he was drawn upwards and began to whirl through the sky. The delightful feeling that he remembered from his previous journey with the Wind, returned to him and, as he swirled and turned and twisted among the stars, the faces of Ver and Aestas, Autumnus and Hiems spun around him and he fell into a dreaming state which lasted a thousand years. He smiled to himself and stretched out his arms towards something of exquisite, indescribable beauty which he knew was there, and yet he didn't know what it was — and found himself clutching a soft blanket.

He opened his eyes with a start. He was lying fully

clothed on his own bed, in his own house, in London. The window was open and banging to and fro with the force of the wind raging outside. He got up quickly and closed it in case the noise woke someone up. It was black and cold outside and the snow shone with a dull whiteness from the trees and roofs. He looked at the library clock ticking beside his bed. The hands pointed to a quarter past midnight and as he looked at it, it chimed in its soft familiar voice. On the bed lay the bag he had used to put the Teapot in. He rushed over to it, pulled the Teapot out and looked inside. For one terrible moment he thought he had fallen asleep and had been dreaming, and all his plans were spoiled. But there, glowing up from the bottom of the bag, was the jewel. Its strong, green light shone out into the room. He heaved a sigh of relief, and then sneezed loudly several times. 'Oh no!' he thought to himself, 'I can't have caught a cold! Now of all times. I'd better get straight into bed and get some sleep.'

So he got undressed quickly, hid the bag with the Teapot and Emerald under the bed, climbed in between the sheets, and blew out the candle. The clock ticked on through the darkness. 'Won't Melissa be pleased,' he thought to himself, and with that, he fell asleep.

He woke up to find daylight pouring into his room, for he'd forgotten to pull the curtains the night before, and sneezed five times. His head felt muzzy and heavy and it was difficult to breathe properly. There was no doubt about it, he had a cold. At that moment there was a knock at the door and Mrs Parkin's head appeared.

'Morning, Sebastian. It's half past eight and you'll be late for your lessons if you don't hurry up.' Then she took a closer look at him. 'My, you don't look well at all.'

And indeed Sebastian was beginning to feel worse and worse. His head ached so much he could hardly bear to move, and his eyes kept watering so that Mrs Parkin's round form looked blurred and wobbly.

'I'b dot feeling too well,' he said, as clearly as he could. 'I think I've got a code.'

'It certainly sounds as if you have, dear,' said Mrs Parkin, in booming tones which went through Sebastian's aching head like knives. 'I think you'd better stay in bed today. I'll bring your breakfast up, and tell Mr Drycrust you're not well enough for your lessons. Dear me, and your father coming home in less than a fortnight, too. Let's hope you're well by then. We don't want him and the new mistress thinking you haven't been looked after properly.'

Sebastian felt rather cross at the suggestion that he wasn't considered to have been looking after himself, but was too interested in what Mrs Parkin had just said, to be annoyed for long. 'Did you say "in less thad a fortdite"? '

'I did so, dearie,' said Mrs Parkin, beaming at him. 'I had a wire this morning saying that they'd be home a week on Tuesday if we could get the rooms ready by then. Which of course we can, as the Master knows.'

Sebastian lay back on the pillow to rest his throbbing head. Less than two weeks till his father came home! That was marvellous, and he suddenly felt very cheerful in spite of his aches and pains. Through a watery blur he watched Mrs Parkin light the fire in his room, and as the flames licked the dry logs and crept over the paper, he gradually drifted off into a doze, and then into a deep sleep.

He woke again in the late afternoon just as it was growing dark. He sat up in bed and was happy to find that his head didn't ache nearly as much and he felt less dizzy. He bent down to look under the bed. Yes, the bag was still there. He wondered if anyone had missed the Teapot yet, and decided that he'd better put it back before awkward questions were asked. Putting on his dressing-gown, he opened the door of his room and, seeing that there was no one around, went down to the kitchen. He put the Teapot in its usual place and went upstairs again. Just as he was passing the foot of the attic stairs he remembered that Melissa still didn't know that he had found the Emerald, so up he went at top speed and in no time at all the Mirror was pouring out smoke. The first thing he saw when the smoke cleared was Melissa's happy face.

'Hallo,' she called before he could speak, 'thank goodness

you're all right. I felt terribly anxious about you facing heaven knows what dangers, and all for me. It's marvellous to see you!'

Sebastian felt quite overcome at her enthusiasm, and thought it was nice of her to be concerned about him, rather than ask straight away about the Emerald.

'Yes, I'b fide,' he said as clearly as he could, 'add I've got the Eberood.'

'What?' said Melissa, 'I say, have you caught a cold? Oh dear, I am sorry.'

'Oh, dote worry,' said Sebastian, 'I think I caught it the other day id the park. It's dot bad, and I dote have to have lessods at the bobent, which is very dice. Adyway, I've got the Eberood.'

'Did you say "Emerald"?' said Melissa, her eyes shining with excitement. 'Oh Sebastian!'

And the happiness in her face made Sebastian feel that the nastiest moment in the Forest had been well worth it.

'What a wonderful day this has been,' said Melissa, 'first, you're back, safe and sound. And then you've found the Emerald—and I can't wait to hear how you did it! And then look what I found this morning by the stream.' And she held up a pair of silver skates. The blades were sharp and delicate, and attached to them were white lacing boots which shimmered all over, as if they had been frosted with silver.

'Aren't they simply beautiful?' she said. 'They were lying on a pile of icicles and I couldn't resist trying them on. They fitted perfectly and I went skating for miles along the stream. I've never skated before but I think there's something special about these skates, for it was so easy, it was almost like flying. I do hope it isn't stealing?' she added anxiously.

'Do, of course dot,' said Sebastian, 'they were beant for you and I cad tell you who they're frob, but it's a very log story add if I dote get back to bed sood, sobody's goig to catch me. We cad talk about everythig toborrow. Thigs are lookig very hopeful, adyway, so dote worry.'

'Oh, I shan't,' she said, grinning happily, 'now that I know you're all right I shan't worry about anything. Go back to bed and get better quickly and I shall think of all the questions I'm going to ask you. I'm dying to know what happened. Thank you very much, Sebastian, you are wonderful.'

Sebastian felt rather embarrassed and said that it was perfectly all right, and anyone could have done it, and anyway he had had help. They said goodbye and then the mist closed over the glass again.

Sebastian went back to bed, and not a moment too soon, for just as he pulled the blankets round him he heard Mrs Parkin's tea-tray.

'Ah good,' she said, 'I'm glad to see you're awake. Feeling better now?'

'Buch, thank you,' said Sebastian, 'I think I'b albost well dow,' and he sneezed loudly.

'Hm, I'm not sure about that,' she said. 'Anyway you must be hungry after missing breakfast and lunch, so eat up.'

She poured his tea and stoked the fire up. Then she sat down on the bed and they discussed the arrangements for his father's homecoming. It was very pleasant, with the fire crackling away, and he soon made up for not having eaten anything that day. Then, when the tray had been taken away, he curled up with a book. It was about a man who went hunting for animals in the African jungle. He had lots of adventures and Sebastian enjoyed the book, but he couldn't help thinking that his own adventures were rather exciting, and much more extraordinary. He decided that when he was older he would write a book about the strange things that had happened to him.

The next day Sebastian's head was a good deal clearer and he managed to eat a large breakfast. When he'd finished it, he tried to think of something to do. It was very dull lying in bed, and his room was too high to see much out of the window except for a patch of grey, cloudy sky. There were lots of books beside his bed but he didn't feel like reading.

By lunch time he was very bored and cross, so Mrs Parkin suggested that he go down to the library and do some painting. This seemed a good idea, he'd forgotten about painting in the excitement of the last two weeks. He got dressed quickly and found some paper and his paint-box. Then it occurred to him that now might be a good time to go and talk to Melissa, before he got too involved with his picture. He climbed the stairs to the attic, feeling much less wobbly and dizzy than he had the day before.

It was cold and bleak that day, and the wind lifted the tiles on the roof and howled against the window panes. Sebastian felt quite shivery. Soon Melissa appeared before him in the Mirror and he was pleased to see that she wasn't looking at all sad or bored.

'How's your cold?' she asked as soon as she saw him.

'Much better, thank you,' said Sebastian. 'I'm just terribly bored. I can't think how you've managed to spend all that time by yourself, without going mad with boredom.'

'Oh well, the first fifty years were the worst. I just used to make up games and things, and try out all the magic I could find. This house is so enormous that there's a lot of exploring to do, too. Then there's the garden and things. It wasn't too bad when I got used to it, although of course I was pretty miserable. Look, I've got an idea. Why don't you come over here? It's about a week since you came last so I think the Teapot would work again. You can't make magic objects work too often, you know, they get very tired and then they stop working altogether. I should think it would be all right, now.'

'Anyway, I've got the Emerald,' said Sebastian. 'Wouldn't that work? It's supposed to be more powerful than the Teapot after all.'

'Shhh,' said Melissa, looking quite nervous. 'You'll offend the Teapot dreadfully if you say things like that. Magic objects are awfully proud, you know. It would think that you didn't appreciate its efforts last time, if you don't use it again.'

'All right,' said Sebastian, 'the Teapot it is. It's a jolly good idea anyway, because then I can tell you all about the people I met and everything, and we can make plans for what to do next. See you soon then.'

'Right,' said Melissa, 'goodbye.'

And the mist was back, moving slowly through the cold air.

Sebastian went down to the library and laid out his painting things. He had no idea how long he would have to wait before the Teapot would work and so he thought he might as well fill in time by starting a picture for his father. Two hours later when Mrs Parkin brought in the tea-tray, he was working busily and had almost forgotten about the plans he and Melissa had made, he was enjoying himself so much. It was getting dark quickly now and Mrs Parkin made tut-tutting noises about the poor light and him ruining his eyes. She was just putting down the tray in order to light the lamps, when the Teapot toppled over and fell into the hearth.

'Goodness me,' said Mrs Parkin, 'what a good thing it didn't go on the carpet. I shall have to go and make another pot, though. Oh well, can't be helped, I suppose,' and she went clucking down to the kitchen. And, as

Sebastian sat there, watching the firelight flickering on the walls, he saw that it had grown very dark indeed, without him noticing. Shadows loomed tall and mysterious round the room. Some of them looked rather like human beings, in fact, when he looked carefully, he was sure that he could see heads and arms and legs. And, even as he watched, something strange was happening. A particularly tall shadow which stood in one corner, was moving of its own accord. A dark patch which was roughly the shape of a man came gliding across the carpet towards him. He could see right through the drifting shadow, and, in spite of all his experience of extraordinary happenings, he felt quite alarmed. As the shadow reached him it spoke, and its voice was muffled, as if it were wrapped in a blanket.

'Hold my hand, Sebastian, and light the lamps.'

Sebastian blinked and then put out his hand towards the point where the shadow's arm dissolved in the firelight. He felt something close round it. It was like burying your hand into thick soft fur.

'That's right,' came the muffled voice again, 'now the lamps.'

Sebastian politely pointed out that he needed two hands to light a match. The shadow heaved a sigh. Then it bent down to the fireplace and, plunging its arm right into the depths of the fire, it pulled out a single flame, which leaped and danced on the invisible hand. At this point, in the bright firelight, the shadow was hardly visible, but Sebastian could feel that he was definitely holding something. He felt himself being pulled over to the lamps which hung on the wall, and, as they moved into the darker part of the room, the shadow appeared again and the flame jumped and spat in its hand.

'I say, you're not going to burn yourself, are you?' Sebastian asked anxiously.

'Of course not,' said the muffled voice, 'I'm only a

shadow. Now, as I hold the flame to the lamp, you turn the gas up, and don't let go, whatever happens.'

Sebastian did as he was told, and, as the gas began to burn, the room grew lighter and lighter and all the shadows began to creep back into the walls and behind the books. Sebastian found himself being tugged over to the wall and suddenly realized with a shock that he was expected to go through it just as the shadows did.

'Just a moment,' he said hastily. 'I don't want to be awkward but I don't really think...' and then he broke off in astonishment for half his body had disappeared from sight into the wall and then the room vanished and he was through. He found himself outside in the open air and slithering down the wall of his house as easily as if he did it every day of his life. He landed smoothly on the pavement and looked around him quickly, hoping that no one had seen him arriving in such an odd way. Fortunately the street was empty.

'There!' said the shadow, 'that wasn't painful, was it? Now we'd better get going. It won't take long as we can go straight there. How do you like being a shadow, by the way?'

'Being a shadow?' said Sebastian, and looked down at himself.

Sure enough, where his legs should have been there was a dark, wavering shape, and he could see the pavement through his feet.

'Well,' he thought to himself, 'I shall never be surprised at anything after this. It's very pleasant,' he said to the dark patch beside him.

'Good,' came the reply, 'come on then. Keep hold of my hand and we'll be there in no time.'

Sebastian drifted down the street with his companion.

'I say, I didn't know that shadows could walk about and all that sort of thing.'

'Well, we don't often as it happens,' said his shadowy friend. 'We're rather a lazy bunch and like to sleep most of the time in dark corners. We're active in bright sunlight but then of course you can't see us.'

'I see,' said Sebastian, 'and can you take any shape you like?'

'Of course we can. It would be difficult to find somewhere to lie down if we couldn't. You can't relax by a table if you look like a chair, now can you?'

'No, I suppose not,' murmured Sebastian, thinking hard. It was surprising how little one knew about the ordinary, familiar things that one had grown up with. At this point they had reached the end of the street, but instead of turning the corner as Sebastian expected, he was led firmly over to the house opposite and straight through the wall.

'Follow me and keep close to the edge,' whispered the shadow.

Sebastian found that he walked right into someone's drawing-room. Several people were sitting round talking to each other and laughing, and they took no notice of the two shadows gliding along the walls. They passed out of the room and through the house. Along a corridor they met a young maid coming straight towards them. Sebastian pulled back without thinking, but the furry grasp on his hand tightened and he was pulled straight through her. She carried on down the corridor and didn't seem to have noticed anything. In no time at all they had come through the other side of the house and were in the open air again. They walked on a little way and then plunged into another house. Sebastian was enjoying himself. It was great fun to be able to see other people without them being able to see him. He had often wondered what it would be like to be invisible. They kept walking straight ahead, through houses and shops and streets and people for several miles. It wasn't tiring though for they could glide very quickly, and there was so much to look at. Eventually they came into countryside and passed through fields and hedges and trees. They were going at quite a speed now and it was difficult to talk because of the howling wind, but Sebastian didn't feel cold, it was as if he was wrapped from head to toe in a great furry coat. He noticed that the countryside around him was beginning to change and the trees became thicker and more tangled. It was dark but not frightening. He supposed this was because a shadow was part of the darkness, and one couldn't very well be afraid of oneself. The only thing that was sinister was the brooding melancholy you sensed as you passed through the trees. The further they went, the stronger this became, almost as if the trees were alive like people.

At last they came to the great iron gate which was the entrance to Melissa's prison. They slid through it with ease and drifted across the garden. Here, the shadow deliberately avoided going through the trees. 'Don't want to get tangled up with that lot,' he said firmly, 'very strong they are.' Sebastian wanted to ask him what he meant, but at that moment they arrived at the front door.

'See you later,' said the shadow and he let go of Sebastian's hand and slithered off into the darkness. Sebastian suddenly felt cold, and looking down, he saw that he was back to normal. 'Oh well,' he thought, 'no use trying to go through things any more.' He climbed up the steps to the great door and it opened before him at once. This time the orange cat was waiting for him. He was sitting at the end of the corridor washing himself. The candles flickered in the heavy silence and threads of blue smoke curled round Sebastian's head as he made his way forward. Mantari watched him with yellow unblinking eyes and then began to purr. When Sebastian reached him the cat rubbed himself to and fro against his legs, mewing and

purring all the time. Sebastian realized that Mantari somehow knew of his adventure and that the Emerald had been
found, and he was very approving.

'Hallo Mantari,' he said, bending down to stroke him.
'I'm pleased to see you, too. Shall we go and find Melissa?'

The cat blinked at him in the candlelight and then set off in front at a slow pace. This time Sebastian had no difficulty in following him and it wasn't long before he had arrived at the gold and silver room and was saying 'hallo' to Melissa.

'I'm so glad you got here all right. It's lovely to see you,' Melissa said, happily, 'come and sit down and let's have tea.'

Very soon there was a marvellous spread before them. Hot chocolate and curranty buns and a large pink cake, not forgetting, of course, pieces of turkey and milk for Mantari. They ate and talked, and Sebastian told her of his strange journey there, as a shadow. Then, when they had finished tea, he told her what had happened when he'd said the poem to summon the Wind, and how he'd found himself in the Cave of the Seasons, and how they'd taken him to the Grey Forest. Then he told her what had happened in the Forest itself, how narrowly he'd escaped its enchantment, and how his friends had helped him. Melissa heard it all in wonder, she was fascinated and terrified.

'It sounds very frightening,' she said, wide-eyed with amazement. 'I know I couldn't have done it, even with the Seasons to help me. I think you were terribly brave and I'll never forget what you've done.'

Sebastian felt himself starting to go pink at this, and hastily went on to tell her that the skates she had found in the garden were from Hiems.

'Oh, yes,' said Melissa, very pleased, 'I suppose they must have been. Oh, I do wish I'd been able to meet them all. Still, I've never done anything to deserve it anyway.'

'Oh, yes you have,' said Sebastian, 'I think you've been jolly cheerful and brave about living on your own all this time. Hiems must have thought so, too. That's why he gave you the present.'

Melissa felt very happy about this and after some more talking, during which she told him about the visit from the Enchanter, they went down to the Room of Books. Sebastian had told Melissa about the man he had found asleep in the Forest, and of Hiems' suggestion, and she was very anxious to find a way to help him.

They searched the Book from cover to cover, which took them hours, but found nothing which seemed to be of any help. There were hundreds of strange and exciting spells, but the children were much too sensible to try them. It is a great mistake to dabble in magic without good reason, as they both knew. At last they decided to give it up for, as Melissa pointed out, last time the Book had shown them what to do, and as it obviously didn't want to show them now, it would be much better to wait until the time was right.

'Let's see if it will help us to get to the Enchanter's garden instead,' suggested Melissa. And just as she said it, the Book, which had lain trembling in her hands, leapt into the air and came down with a crash on to the floor, where it lay hissing and pouring out green smoke. The pages fluttered over and over and came to a stop at a chapter which they hadn't seen before, although they had searched right through the Book. It was called 'To summon the Steeds of the Enchanter', and went as follows:

'He who desires to enter the secret realm of the Enchanter may find it only by summoning the Enchanter's Steeds. No man could find his way alone to the hidden garden, should he search for a thousand years!'

'This is it then,' said Sebastian, unnecessarily.

They continued to read. 'To summon the Steeds. He who

desires it, must possess a Power Object and a loving heart.'

'Well we can manage the first,' said Sebastian, 'what do you think about the second, Melissa?' and he grinned at her.

'Stop interrupting,' she said, sternly. But she wasn't really cross. 'Let's get on. "Any of the five Objects will do but it is preferable to use the most powerful." That's the Emerald for us, I should think,' she added, forgetting what she had said about not interrupting. ' "He must then gather branches from any trees which possess a spirit and build a fire. When it is burning strongly the Object must be thrown into the heart of the flames and the following poem said. The number of Steeds required should be clearly stated." '

'Well,' said Melissa, as they sat back and looked at one another. 'Where do we find trees which possess a spirit?'

Sebastian thought for a moment. 'When I passed

through some of the trees on my way here today, the nearer I got to the house the stranger the trees felt. Sort of alive and brooding. I wouldn't be a bit surprised if they had spirits. I should think the trees from this garden would do for the fire actually. The shadow said they were the strongest of all.'

'Good heavens. Fancy having lived here for ninety-nine years and not realized that,' said Melissa, 'I must say I've always felt those trees weren't like ordinary trees but it never occurred to me that they were...well, alive.'

'A very odd idea, isn't it?' said Sebastian. 'Let's hope I'm right, anyway. What does the poem say?'

Melissa read it out and it went as follows:

> I call, majestic beast,
> Shake your flowing mane
> And gallant proud-arched neck,
> And hear my gentle summons
> For a mighty noble steed,
> A royal snow-white bearer,
> A valiant speeding arrow,
> I call. Hear me and appear.

'How do we change that to get two?' wondered Sebastian. 'Oh, I know. We just add s's on the end of words like mane and beast and ask for "Two royal snow-white bearers" and so on.'

'Do you think the poem will work if we change it?' asked Melissa anxiously.

'Well, it did say that the number we wanted should be clearly stated, and it sounds rather silly to ask for one in the poem and then say "Could we have another one please," doesn't it?'

'Yes, I suppose so. Let's write it down then.'

Melissa had remembered this time to bring a pencil and paper down with her just in case, so they soon had the poem written down and the Book was put back on the shelf where it belonged. The children decided to go upstairs and have something more to drink while they made their plans. (This was Sebastian's idea for he loved to watch the table produce things out of nothing.)

Over silver cups of a kind of raspberry juice they decided that Sebastian should come to the Treasure House as soon as the Teapot would work, bringing the Emerald and the Teapot with him. They weren't sure what to do about the Mirror as they had no idea what way the Teapot would choose to get him there, and it wasn't possible to carry the Mirror all the way on foot.

'Perhaps the mirror here would work,' suggested Melissa, 'after all it's really only one mirror with two faces.'

'I suppose it might,' agreed Sebastian, 'I'll think about it over the next few days. We don't want to make a silly mistake at this stage.'

'I wish we'd been able to do something for that poor man in the Forest,' said Melissa. 'Perhaps the Book will be able to come up with something later.' And she suddenly gave an enormous yawn.

'Time for me to go home,' said Sebastian. 'I'll learn the poem as soon as possible and why don't you learn it too? It will give you something to do and it would be just as well to make sure.'

'All right,' said Melissa and then she got up to go down to the front door with him.

They walked through the hundreds of corridors with Mantari, who kept hiding round corners and darting out at their feet.

'He's getting very kittenish these days,' said Melissa. 'I do hope that if I ever get out of here, he'll be able to live with me then as well. I couldn't bear not to know what had happened to him.'

'Don't worry,' said Sebastian, 'it'll all sort itself out somehow,' and at that moment there was a low growl of thunder.

Melissa looked pale. 'I didn't like the sound of that at all,' she said nervously, 'that wasn't an ordinary clap of thunder. I think the Enchanter is getting suspicious. Oh, I do hope the Teapot works quickly!'

'Me too,' said Sebastian. He didn't fancy having to deal with the Enchanter face to face, one bit.

As they came to the front door they said goodbye, and then Melissa went up to her rose and silver bedroom, and Sebastian went out into the night. As he stepped under the black, starless sky, the shadow rose up from the stone steps and took Sebastian's hand. He felt the warm furry feeling creep over him. A tug on his hand led him over to the dark trees. Together he and the shadow slipped through the garden and walked straight through an enormously high wall which surrounded it. Indeed it was so high that Sebastian couldn't see the top. Soon they were speeding through the countryside. The journey back was without events, for the shadow seemed too exhausted to talk. The further they went the lighter it got, until they were drifting through London in the dusk of a late winter afternoon. At last they passed through the front door of Sebastian's own house. Just as they were about to go up the stairs, the shadow whispered a muffled 'goodbye', let go of Sebastian's hand and lay down on one of the steps. Sebastian saw that he had become an ordinary human boy once more, so he dashed up the stairs like lightning and had just sat down in his chair as Mrs Parkin came in, carrying the Teapot.

'Oh good,' she said, 'I'm glad you've lit the lamps. Thank you very much, dear.'

Sebastian thought that if she'd known who had really lit them, she would have been very surprised indeed.

As Sebastian slept through the black, snowy, London night, far away in another world (much farther in fact than either of them knew) Melissa dozed peacefully in her bedroom at the Treasure House. As she lay sleeping, the orange cat cuddled in the crook of her knees, she began to dream. She dreamed that she was standing in the Grey Forest, and it was just as Sebastian had described it to her. It rose up around her, dark and terrifying, and even the glorious crimson of her dress had turned a drab, dirty grey. The heavy air ruffled her hair and lifted the drooping leaves in dank, warm gusts. Lying on the ground, a few yards from where she was standing, was an old, old man. He was sleeping heavily, but as she watched him he stirred a little and groaned, as if he were in pain. She crept closer and saw that his grey cheeks were washed with tears which ran down his face and soaked into his long, matted beard. Melissa felt like crying too, for she knew that this was the man Sebastian had told her about, who was doomed to sleep for ever in this place worse than death. The man slumbered on, crying out from time to time, but unable to wake. Suddenly a long shadow fell across him and looking up Melissa saw a man standing in the gloom, dressed from head to foot in deep purple. His evil was so strong that even the Forest could not pale his body to grey. His face was knotted in a smile of malice and hatred.

As she stood watching, the evil figure bent over the helpless sleeper and stretched down a dreadful, spiny hand to touch the man's forehead. Melissa shook with fear, but a courage she had never before dreamed she possessed, forced her to move forward and put out her small, grey hand to shield him.

'Leave him alone,' she cried. 'Don't touch him. He is unhappy enough. You're not to hurt him.'

And she took hold of the evil hand and pulled it away. A shudder ran through her as she touched it and she felt the terrible agony of fear and loneliness. She held it tightly though her hand seemed to burn in its clasp. She leaned over the sleeping body and covered it with the folds of her dress. A dreadful scream of anger tore through the Forest.

'Who are you who dares to challenge Nightmare?' hissed the cruel mouth and his eyes burned her as she looked into them. 'This man belongs to me. You cannot help him.'

'I'm not afraid of you,' cried Melissa, and her voice was angry too. 'You are a coward to hurt who cannot help himself.'

Nightmare laughed. A terrible shrieking laugh which made the trees tremble and bend their branches to the ground. Melissa felt her blood run cold and a wave of panic swept through her, but the groans of the sleeping man filled her with rage against this creature who could cause such misery. Nightmare shook off her hand as easily as if he were brushing away a feather. He stretched his fingers towards her throat. She wanted desperately to run, but she could not leave the man alone with this monster. As his bony, needle-like fingers closed around her neck and seared her flesh, she screamed aloud. 'You're a coward. You can't hurt me. You're only a dream!'

As she said this, she felt the hands loosen around her throat and her veins began to throb with blood again. Nightmare stepped back and a tremor passed through his body

'A dream! A dream!' she shouted again.

The Nightmare began to quiver and change. Tongues of white fire licked up from the hem of his black robe and consumed his body. As the purple flesh fell in charred flakes from his face, his skin took on the hue of frosted marble, and hair began to grow from his head in soft, white curls. A long beard rippled down from his chin, and his robes, now white, hung shimmering to the ground. His eyes shone with a profound peace and serenity, and the face of the sleeping man grew tranquil.

'I am Sleep,' said the stranger, in a slow, deep voice. 'Nightmare is banished through your courage and you shall have your reward.'

He bent over the sleeping man and touched him lightly on the forehead.

'Awake! Your sleep is over.'

And, as he said that, the man opened his eyes and he smiled. He rose to his feet and the years fell away from him and he stood, full of life and strength, a young man again. Where he had lain a small, white flower grew and cast its light into the shadows. The young man bent down and plucked the flower and, as he did so, the tree under which he had slept for so many years, began to droop and wither. The young man gave the flower to Melissa and then his body began to grow translucent and fade, and with a cry of ecstasy, he vanished.

'He has gone back to the past, to his own time and his own people, and to find happiness again,' said Sleep. 'He has suffered enough for his moment of weakness.'

Then Sleep took Melissa by the hand and led her through the Forest. She saw trees curling and dying around her, and here and there bloomed white flowers like the one she held in her hand. A sudden breeze began to blow, a cool, fresh wind which stirred the sickly odour of the tepid air. Melissa took a deep breath, and the pure air which rushed into her lungs made her flesh tingle and eyes sparkle. Overhead patches of blue sky appeared, gaining in size and depth of colour at every moment. As the strips of bark peeled from the dying trees, threads of brown and green and purple ran up the smooth, bare trunks, swallowing the greyness. Along the ground rivers of green and yellow and russet ran like quick-silver through the dark undergrowth, flickering over the bracken and tingeing it with gold and flame, leaping up the grass-stalks, staining them emerald and filling them with life and sweetness. And suddenly the silence was broken by a shrill burst of song. Flying through the trees towards them was a golden bird, followed by a flock of brown and white and speckled birds, blackbirds and bluebirds, filling the air with their joyful chirping and twittering.

Melissa turned to Sleep, who was smiling at her bewilderment.

'Time has come back to the Forest,' he said. 'Look!'

Melissa followed the direction of his pointing finger and saw, darting in and out among the trees, the slight, tall figure of a woman, whose dress was a sheet of flowers, whose skin was like petals, whose hair was a mass of long, curling feathers. She dipped and swayed among the bushes and trees and undergrowth, and wherever she laid her hand, things burst into life.

'Why, it's Spring!' cried Melissa.

'Yes,' came the voice beside her, and it was even deeper than before.

Melissa found that the hand she held belonged to a very tall man whose white skin shot out sparks of silver as he moved, who wore a cloak of ermine and whose eyes were turquoise ice, and saw into her very soul. His crown of icicles glittered in the bright sunlight. Her heart beat with joy at the thought that one of her dearest wishes had been fulfilled. She had seen the great god Winter. In her dream he smiled at her, and then released her hand with a sign that she was to go on.

Before her Sleep stood veiled in a curtain of golden light, and beckoned her. She walked forward and the golden light dissolved around her and brushed her cheek softly.

A little farther off she saw another curtain this time of silver. Sleep beckoned her on again, and as she passed through it, it left a silver mist, like tiny diamonds, on her skin. Before her hung a veil of tear-drops, spinning with every colour of the rainbow, and as she touched it, it broke into bubbles and she awoke in her bedroom at the Treasure House with the white flower in her hand.

As soon as she saw Sebastian in the Mirror the next morning, she told him about her dream and showed him the flower. He was very excited about it and begged her again and again to describe exactly what had happened. He was thrilled that another of their adventures had turned out successfully and felt that this boded well for their next and probably last adventure, which was perhaps the most dangerous of all. Finding the green Rose of the Enchanter.

They discussed their plans and talked away until the Mirror faded and it was time for lunch.

The days that followed were happy ones for Melissa. She put the flower in a crystal bowl beside her bed where it shone out a gentle light even at night-time. Each day its delicate petals gave out a sweet scent and its glowing centre showered the table with yellow pollen dust. Every time she looked at it, she thought to herself, 'Well, even if this does all come to nothing, it won't have been a waste of time. At least no one will ever be caught by the Grey Forest again!'

And this thought made her feel very happy and quite hopeful for her own freedom.

Sebastian spent the next few days walking in the park (for his cold was almost gone now) and painting a picture for his father. The thought of seeing him again made him feel very excited and impatient for the days to pass. The snow continued to fall from time to time and he spent many happy hours trudging through it, and sliding on the frozen puddles. Mrs Parkin and the others were good-tempered and cheerful for they all liked and respected the 'Master' and were all very curious to meet the new 'Missus'. He spent long afternoons in the kitchen, chatting with Mrs Parkin, and the Latin lessons, which had now begun again, didn't seem nearly as dull as they had before. And all the time he wondered, and waited, and watched the Teapot where it sat on the shelf above the kitchen range.

That Sunday, two days before his father was expected to arrive back from India, Sebastian came down to the kitchen to see what everyone else was doing. He had spent the early part of the day making sure that he knew the summoning poem perfectly, and had said it over and over again until he couldn't possibly make a mistake. Now he wanted someone to talk to. Unhappily he found that Mrs Parkin and Sarah were getting ready to go to church. Sebastian never went himself for he didn't understand the service and so there really wasn't much point in going and feeling fidgety and spoiling it for everyone else. He resigned himself to an afternoon with a book, and a large tea when they came back.

Mrs Parkin stuck her hat-pin in firmly, as if she were skewering a joint of meat, and her face beamed out from under a collection of shiny glass beads and fruit. It was a wonderful hat. It wobbled dangerously and clinked and rattled as she talked. Sarah has a smaller, less colourful hat, but this was because she was younger. They pulled on their long black gloves and clattered out of the house, Williams and Sylvester solemnly walking behind them, in stiff high collars and black suits. Their boots shone and their faces glowed.

The house seemed very quiet after they'd gone. It was

only half past two and they wouldn't be back until at least half past three. Sebastian was just thinking about going upstairs again, to find a book, when a gruff voice broke the silence and made him jump.

'Look sharp, then,' it said, 'let's get going.'

Sebastian looked round. The kitchen was quite empty but for himself.

'Come on then!' said the gruff voice again. 'Don't stand there dreaming. I'm up here.'

Sebastian looked up and saw the Teapot staring down at him, and clucking impatiently.

'Well,' it said, 'are we going or aren't we? If you've changed your mind you ought to have said so before. I've quite worn myself out, working up my strength for this. All that hot tea inside me as well. It doesn't help you know, it doesn't help one bit.'

Sebastian found his tongue. 'Of course I haven't changed my mind. Just tell me what to do and we can go at once.'

'Right then,' said the Teapot, 'lift me down from the shelf, get the Emerald and take us both up to the Mirror. And don't forget to bring some matches. Come on, boy. You don't look very pretty, standing there with your mouth open, you know. Not pretty at all.'

Sebastian privately thought the Teapot was rather rude but he did as he was told. He took the Teapot down and found some matches by the stove. Then he went up to his bedroom and got the Emerald out of the bag under his bed, and climbed the stairs to the attic. When they were standing in front of the Mirror the Teapot began to mutter to it, in a strange language. Sebastian couldn't understand a word of it. After about five minutes of this, the Teapot suddenly opened and shut its lid with a great crash, and then the Mirror began to pour out clouds of green smoke as usual. Sebastian was just about to take hold of the handles when the Teapot shouted out, 'Don't touch it! Dear me, you'll spoil everything at this rate. Now do as I say. Push the Emerald and me through the Mirror and climb through yourself. Don't touch the handles, whatever happens. Now do hurry up, I can't keep this up for ever, you know.'

It passed through Sebastian's mind, at this point, that he had once read a book about a girl called Alice who had gone through a mirror, so he supposed it could be done. Ah, but hadn't it turned out that she had been dreaming anyway? He couldn't make his mind up about it, and the Teapot was making such impatient noises by now that he thought he'd better get on with it. He pulled over a chair from the corner, and stood on it, pushed the Teapot and the Emerald into the smoke and let them go. They disappeared with a loud clang, presumably having fallen to the ground the other side. It didn't seem to be difficult to get through, anyway, so he stretched out his hand into the glass and felt nothing but cold air. Cautiously he swung one leg through. It was difficult to see now, as the smoke was going in his eyes and wrapping itself round his head, so he just held on to the frame (being careful not to touch the handles), brought the other leg through, and jumped to the floor the other side.

When the smoke cleared Sebastian saw that Melissa was standing in front of him and he was in the gold and silver room of the Treasure House. The Teapot and the Emerald lay at his feet and Mantari was walking in circles around them, miaowing and looking very pleased.

'Phew. That's better!' said the Teapot, and his voice, instead of sounding gruff, was silvery. 'I'm sorry I was rather bad-tempered. It was the strain of getting the magic right, and the Treasure House was pulling me so hard that I began to feel quite ill. You're quite right about the cat of course, he's eaten the Silver Fish all right. You can use the Mirror on this side for the Well, it's quite strong enough on it's own. My word, it's good to be here at last.'

Sebastian turned round to look at the Mirror. It had stopped smoking now and the glass was hard and cold to touch.

'Well done, Teapot,' he said, to show that he had quite forgiven it for being niggly. 'How did you manage it?'

But the Teapot was silent, and Sebastian never heard it speak again.

'I expect it was all part of that particular piece of magic,' said Melissa, sadly. She would have liked to have had a chat with it and find out how it did things. 'I must say I really couldn't think what was happening when it came thumping into the room and the Emerald after. It

gave me such a shock. Then it explained to me what was going on while you were coming through. Let's put it in a safe place and go out and build a fire. Have you learnt the poem?'

'Yes,' replied Sebastian, 'I think I've got it perfectly now. I'll bring the Emerald in my pocket.'

So the two of them, with the cat whisking along in front, went out into the garden. It was dusk now and a slight wind stirred the cold air and made the leaves tremble. They began to gather all the fallen branches and twigs they could find, and pile them up into a bonfire. It was soon quite high.

Then Sebastian got out the matches and struck one. It fizzled a bit, and didn't seem to want to burn, but, before it could die, he held it under a dry twig which he had carefully picked out. It caught light at once and burned with a strange whistling noise almost like singing. He threw it into the centre of the heap and it burst into flames at once. The noise was tremendous. All the branches began to whistle and sing, and all on different notes. And to Sebastian and Melissa, standing side by side in the damp, cold air, the smell of wood smoke hanging around them, it seemed that magic was indeed at work again, and that this would be their biggest adventure yet. The flames were purple and bright blue.

When they were jumping really high, Sebastian took a careful aim and threw the Emerald deep into the blaze. Then he and Melissa began to chant the poem together. They had to shout to hear themselves above the whistling, but as soon as they came to an end, the noise died down and a hush fell over the garden. Even the trees seemed to be watching and listening. Sebastian and Melissa looked at the fire, waiting for something to happen. The Emerald glowed and shone, brighter and brighter, and then it began to grow. From the size of an orange it grew to the size of a melon, and then to the size of a pumpkin, and by this time it was so brilliant that it dazzled them to look at it. Then great sparks of lime green fire shot out all around it and they stepped back in alarm, rather worried that things might be getting out of hand. Suddenly the Emerald shattered into thousands of tiny pieces which seemed to flow upwards and drift into a huge twisting spiral rising from the heart of the fire. It spun at a tremendous speed and, as it did so, all the colours you have ever imagined ran through it and it glittered and shimmered, brighter than any sun. At last it seemed to have exhausted itself for the spiral got lower and lower and then gradually faded out. The children crept forward for a closer look. The flames had gone out and all that was left was a pile of white ashes and a few blackened branches. Right in the middle lay the Emerald, round and green and as perfect as ever. It was very quiet in the garden. Sebastian and Melissa held their breaths and looked around them. At first it seemed as if nothing was going to happen. Then Melissa, who had been staring hard at the Emerald, beckoned to Sebastian to come and look, and said, in a voice which trembled with suppressed excitement, 'there's something moving in the ashes round the Emerald. Do come and see, I'm sure there is!'

Sebastian looked to where her finger was pointing and saw that there was indeed something moving. Something was pushing its way up from the ground, something round and white with two black holes at the top and which grew larger every second. It wasn't until two fine pointed ears came up that they realized what it was. Then came a long curving neck and a heavy white mane. Then a foreleg appeared, strong and graceful and then another. Finally it put both hooves on the ground and pulled itself up. Before them, shaking its mane and brushing the ash from its body with a tail which swept right to the ground, stood a pure white stallion. It lifted its head and whinnied, its call echoing through the twilight air, and the trees bowed their heads meekly in answer. Sebastian and Melissa were so startled and delighted, watching this noble animal, that it was some time before they noticed that another one was rising from the ashes. Before long it stood beside its partner, stamping the ground and shaking its head, every bit as proud and magnificent.

'I say!' said Sebastian, 'aren't they beautiful! The only thing is, I don't know how to ride.'

'Neither do I,' said Melissa, 'but we can't let that stop us now. Let's have a go.'

She picked up the Emerald from the ashes and gave it to Sebastian. He put it in his pocket, then went over to one of the horses and put up his hand to stroke its nose. Then he thought that it might be rather insulting to such a great horse, so he hesitated and put it down again. The stallion bent his head over Sebastian and blew at his hair. Then, very gently, it bit one of his cold pink ears. Sebastian felt that this was the sign that the stallion had accepted him and it was quite safe to mount, and so he struggled undignifiedly up on to the broad white back. He felt very wobbly and it looked an awful long way to the ground. He clung on to the thick, tangled mane and tried to get his balance. The horse stood very patiently for him and didn't seem to mind having someone clamber on to him so clumsily. In fact he seemed to think it was rather funny for he kept bending his head round to have a look and then neighing softly almost as if he were laughing. Melissa managed it a little better, although her long dress got in the way rather, but at last they were both firmly on. Mantari jumped up behind Melissa, climbed over her shoulder, and settled down in front of her. The mane seemed to get up his nose, for he sneezed once or twice, but he managed to hold it down with his paws and at last they were ready to go. They set off at a smooth walk through the garden in the opposite direction to the iron gate. They quickly got used to being so far from the ground and were soon talking and laughing excitedly. Mantari was the only one who didn't seem to enjoy it, but he clung on determinedly, now and then giving a little mew of protest. Then they saw in front of them the vast wall which marked the boundary to the Treasure House gardens. The horses paused for a moment, shook their heads and then broke into a trot, which quickly changed to a canter and then a gallop. They fled over the ground at the speed of the wind and the wall grew larger at every moment. Sebastian, Melissa and the cat crouched low over the white necks and clung on for dear life. Just as the wall loomed right above their heads and seemed about to engulf them in its stony arms, they were airborne and flying over it. They all left their insides behind them and swooped to the ground the other side, feeling giddy and shaking all over, half with excitement and half with terror. They swept on without slowing the pace and the trees whipped past so quickly that they were just a green blur. Melissa's long hair was flung into her face and tangled over her eyes and her dress flowed out behind her like a red flag.

The cat's whiskers, like his ears, were blown flat against his head and when Melissa bent over him to make sure that he was all right, she saw that his eyes were tight shut. Sebastian and Melissa enjoyed the ride, it was exciting to travel at such a speed and to hear the pounding of the hooves, beating time with their hearts. They jumped wide rivers and tall hedges, crossed large fields in a few strides, galloped up hills and down dales, and the stallions never checked their pace for a moment.

At last, though, they began to slow down, and gradually came to a standstill. Mantari continued to crouch with his eyes shut and it wasn't until Melissa had jumped down and taken him in her arms that he dared to open his eyes and straighten his ears and whiskers. Then he leapt to the ground and shook himself, and brushed himself into shape again with his paws. When Melissa and Sebastian had got rid of a few of the tangles so that they could see properly, they looked around them. They were in a valley, standing by a group of trees, with green grass and hills all around. The sky was bright blue and birds sang and twittered over their heads. It was very peaceful, just like an English summer afternoon. A steep bank lay on one side of them and it was covered with thick bushes and pale yellow flowers. One of the horses went over to the bank and pulled at some of the branches with his teeth, and, as they fell away, Sebastian and Melissa saw that they hid the entrance to a dark tunnel. Then the horses lifted their heads and whinnied loudly several times. It was clear that this was as far as the children could go on horseback, and that now they must enter the tunnel in the bank.

'Ready?' said Sebastian to Melissa and she nodded, looking rather anxious. Sebastian felt it was up to him to lead the way as he'd had more experience in this kind of thing, and anyway she was a girl. He went over to the tunnel and stepped inside. It was round and low, and the floor, walls and ceiling were just earth threaded with the roots of trees and bushes. It was quite dry, and the air seemed fresh and pure.

'Come on,' he called to Melissa, and turned round to find her right behind him. Something tickled his legs and brushed past him. It was Mantari, now quite recovered from his journey and as bold as ever. Looking back through the entrance, Sebastian could see the horses grazing in the warm afternoon air.

'Let's go then,' he said cheerfully, and set off down the tunnel. They soon turned a corner which meant that daylight no longer came in to the tunnel, and it could have been rather frightening had it not been for Mantari, whose eyes sent out two beams of yellow light in front of them. They went quite a long way without meeting any difficulties at all and then the tunnel started to go downwards and got much narrower. They kept banging their heads on the roof and their backs soon began to ache with having to bend almost double to get through. Mantari padded on in front lighting up the way. He turned round, now and then, to make sure that they were still there, his eyes bright yellow in the darkness. They began to wonder if they might have missed another turning or something, for the tunnel seemed to go further and further down, and it began to get damp. Sebastian put out his hand to touch the wall and it felt very soggy and wet. It became muddy underfoot, and the light from Mantari's eyes showed a gleam of water here and there. Then they could hear it dripping from the ceiling and trickling down the walls. Mantari didn't like it at all, and gave a low growl every time he got splashed. At last they came to some steps, which went down very steeply. They were crumbling away in places and the three of them had to be very careful not to slip. They had been silent for some time now, for they needed all their breath to struggle down the steps. After they'd been going for some time, though, Sebastian stopped suddenly, and Melissa bumped into him.

'I say,' he said, 'what's that strange light down there?'

Melissa had been busy trying to keep her balance and so hadn't been looking ahead at all, but now she saw that below them the darkness was broken by an eerie purple glow, which spread its fingers of light up towards them.

'Gosh, Sebastian,' she said, 'that is odd. I don't like the look of that at all.'

'Me neither,' he replied, 'but we'd better go and have a look.'

They went down towards it. Then Sebastian realized that they'd come to the end of the tunnel and that the purple light was coming in from outside. He turned to look at Melissa, and saw that her face was pale mauve in the glow.

'This must be the Enchanter's garden,' he whispered.

Melissa nodded and took his hand. Mantari jumped on to Sebastian's shoulder and together they stepped out of the tunnel.

The sight which met their eyes was so amazing that it quite took their breaths away, and for a moment they just stood and stared. They were in the strangest and loveliest garden you could ever imagine. A vast purple sky stretched over their heads, bathing with refracted light the rose-coloured lawns that lay beneath it. A great emerald sun traced its slow arc of ascendance against this rich canopy, trailing in its wake a galaxy of stars. Then, as the children watched, it dipped to the horizon and slowly sank, a brilliant crescent which tipped the silver trees with soft viridian. The moon, a disc of burning gold, climbed from the east and followed the path of the sun until it too sank down to the trees and vanished with a last burst of glory. Up rose the sun once more. And, as the two globes circled across the sky, the space between them spattered with stars, the light in the garden changed from purple and emerald to purple and gold, and back again.

In the distance a fountain played, its clear water leaping to the turning spheres, pausing for a moment, then falling in a glinting cataract to the earth. Around the fountain bloomed flowers of white, flushed with pearl. The tight buds trembled and slowly spread their frail petals to the sky, then drooped and scattered on the grass. New buds sprang up, and bloomed, and died. Walking among these opening and shutting flowers were birds the colour of ivory,

trailing feathers of filigree in smooth sweeps over the ground. Now and then they spread their tails into huge fans, and sang to each other in high, sweet voices.

The children walked slowly over the soft grass to the fountain and Melissa plunged her hand into the basin and let the cool water trickle through her fingers. Her crimson dress floated around her and shone out among the brilliant colours of the garden.

'Isn't this the most beautiful thing you've ever seen?'

she said to Sebastian, and he nodded, too overwhelmed to speak.

Mantari jumped down from his shoulder and walked round the fountain, eyeing the birds carefully. They looked rather too large to chase, in fact it was quite possible that they might get the better of him, so he took care not to get too close. The birds went on singing and took no notice of him.

Melissa shook herself out of the dream into which the singing and the sound of splashing water had sent her, and struggled to concentrate on their task.

'Come on, Sebastian,' she said, 'where do you think the Rose could be?'

Sebastian, who had been standing gazing in front of him with a far-away look in his eyes, gradually brought them into focus and, with an obvious effort, pushed his hair back from his face and looked around. In the distance he saw a clump of bushes, covered with saffron and turquoise flowers and from where he was standing they looked rather like roses.

'Let's try over there,' he said, 'my goodness, it's difficult to keep one's mind on anything in this place, isn't it?'

They set off across the pink grass and Mantari followed behind them, turning round now and then to have a last, longing look at the birds. When they reached the bushes they found that they were indeed roses. There were masses of them, and their strong scent filled the childrens' noses and clung to their hair. They pushed their way among the bushes, getting very torn and scratched, and all the time looking for a rose which might be green. It was a tiring and painful business and the bushes seemed to stretch for miles. All the flowers were varying shades of turquoise and saffron yellow and the leaves were frosted silver. There was not a speck of emerald in sight.

'This is useless,' said Sebastian, at last, 'I don't think the

Rose is here at all. We'll have to look somewhere else.'

They pushed their hair back from their hot foreheads with scratched hands, and Mantari, who had been having a terrible time avoiding all the thorns, jumped up on to Sebastian's shoulder. As they stood there feeling cross and rather down-hearted, one of the birds which they had seen earlier by the fountain, came flying over their heads and then came to rest on a bush just a short way away. It sang a few notes to them over and over again in its clear chiming voice and the children listened, enchanted by its loveliness, and forgot about feeling cross. Then Melissa realized that it was trying to tell them something.

'What is it saying?' she asked Sebastian. 'Do listen, I'm sure it's trying to help us.'

Sebastian listened carefully and gradually the words became clear. 'Why, it's singing "Seek in the heart of the Maze, Seek in the heart of the Maze." I was enjoying the song so much that I never thought it might be trying to tell us something. I suppose that's where the Rose is, do you think? Let's see if we can find the maze, anyway.'

They fought their way out of the tiresome rose bushes and reached the soft grass with sighs of relief. The bird suddenly stopped singing and flew into the air again, swept over the trees and out of sight.

'I wonder if he's showing us where it is,' said Melissa, 'it can't do any harm to follow him, I suppose.'

So they trudged off across the lawn, Mantari stalking in front and twitching his ears warily all the time. He didn't seem to like being in the garden very much, as if he sensed that behind the beauty lurked a strong presence of evil. They passed glades of flowers spread thickly under the changing light, all opening and shutting silently, like moving water. Here and there waterfalls plunged from between rocks which glittered like precious stones, into dark bottomless pools. The trees swayed and nodded as if in time to a glorious music which only they could hear. From time to time a bird gave a loud cry and then fell silent. An uneasiness stole into the childrens' hearts. Mantari suddenly bounded off in front of them, rounded a group of trees and disappeared from sight. When they caught up with him, he was sitting by a hedge which stretched tall and straight far into the distance and out of sight. The hedge was a tawny gold and continued quite unbroken except for a small gap where Mantari was sitting.

'This must be it,' said Sebastian and his heart began to beat quickly.

Together, the three of them walked through the gap and found themselves facing another hedge, exactly like the first, but this time without a gap. This meant that they could go either right or left, and after a moment's deliberation, they decided to go left. They walked for what seemed like hours between the two hedges, which continued tall and thick and impenetrable. At last they found themselves back at the entrance, which was not only annoying, it was also very strange, because they were quite certain that they'd been walking in a straight line and hadn't turned any corners anywhere. They were sure that it was the place they had started from, though, for they recognized the bit of garden they had just walked through.

'Bother,' said Sebastian, crossly, 'there must be a way into the maze. Unless, of course, that bird was playing a trick on us.'

'I don't think so,' said Melissa. 'Perhaps we weren't looking hard enough. I tell you what, let's go different ways. You go to the left and I'll go the to right and we can meet up half-way round and perhaps one of us will have found something.'

So they set off in opposite directions, Mantari following Melissa to the right.

Sebastian walked quickly, trailing his hand along the

hedge as he went, to make quite sure that if there was a gap he wouldn't miss it. To his extreme disappointment, he found himself back at the entrance again.

'Oh, bother,' he thought to himself, 'this is the most irritating maze I've ever come across.'

In fact it was the first maze he had ever been in, but he was too annoyed and puzzled to think of that at the time. Then something occurred to him which stopped him feeling annoyed and made him feel terribly worried and anxious instead. If he'd been all the way round the maze and hadn't found an opening anywhere, why hadn't he met Melissa on the way?

When Melissa had set off from the entrance for the second time, she'd decided to go very slowly, and to look back every now and then to keep Sebastian in sight. She was sure that they hadn't turned any corners last time, and she was very puzzled as to how they could have walked right round the maze without doing so. Mantari seemed quite happy to go slowly too. He trotted on just in front of her, sniffing at the hedges, from time to time. When they had gone a little way, she turned round to look for Sebastian and saw him walking along in the distance, his back towards her.

'So far so good,' she thought to herself and turned round again.

The avenue between the two hedges lay before her, straight, and completely empty as far as she could see. Mantari had disappeared. She called him loudly, and her voice startled her as it broke the silence. There was an answering mew from behind the hedge on her left. She walked along a little way and found that there was a gap leading further into the maze. It was very narrow, and difficult to see until you were almost on top of it.

'We must have walked straight past it the first time,'

she thought to herself. 'Won't Sebastian be pleased when he knows I've found it.'

Then she called Mantari again, for she didn't want to go any further without Sebastian. Mantari didn't come, however, he just went on miaowing somewhere out of sight.

'Oh, dear, I'll have to go and fetch him. I hope he isn't hurt or anything.' And so saying, she stepped through the gap into another avenue, just like the first, and the hedge closed silently behind her.

Mantari ran up to her and rubbed himself against her legs.

'Come on, silly,' she said and picked him up.

When she looked for the gap to get out again, and couldn't find it, she began to feel very worried indeed. She called Sebastian's name several times and got no reply. It was very quiet, even the birds were silent.

'I suppose the best thing to do is to keep walking and hope to find another gap further on. It's all so confusing. This maze seems to have a life of its own,' she said to herself.

This thought was not pleasant at all and her heart began to thump uncomfortably as she made her way along between the hedges, calling Sebastian from time to time and hoping to find a gap which would let her out. She soon found her way blocked by a hedge which grew across her path. There was a gap by the side of it, but it led further into the maze, and not out of it. She had learned by now that it was no use trying to go against magic, and she realized that some force was directing her to the centre of the maze. Whether it was a good or evil force she didn't know, but it was obvious that she wasn't going to be allowed to go and find Sebastian.

She followed the avenues, each one she entered exactly like the others, and, as she walked through the gaps which appeared where her path was barred, they closed behind her, so that she had no choice but to go on. She gave up calling Sebastian. Where he was he could not hear her. She noticed that the further she went, the closer grew the hedges and therefore the darker and narrower her path. Sometimes she tried to turn right instead of left when she came to a gap but always she found her path barred and had to turn back. Just when she was beginning to wonder if this horrible maze was sending her round in circles and she would never be able to get out, she came to a place where hedges grew on all sides and formed a square. As she stepped in she was pleased to see that this time the gap didn't close behind her. In the centre of the square grew a tangle of flowers, each one with a centre of white crystals and whose petals hung like glowing pendants, of ruby and sapphire and pearl. They cast a soft light in the clearing and magic trembled in their leaves. But even their beauty was diminished by the flower which swayed on a single, slender stem above them. A perfect rose, the colour of an emerald.

Melissa's heart leapt with excitement and the cat began to purr. She tip-toed over to the rose and put out her hand to pluck it. A low growl of thunder shook the air around her. Mantari flattened his ears and miaowed quietly. Melissa hesitated for a moment and then took hold of the rose and broke the stem. A loud crash shot through the sky above her head. It began to grow dark very quickly, and suddenly it started to rain. Large, green drops of water poured down around her and as they hit the ground, they sizzled and spat and turned into a green vapour. The vapour snaked up from the ground and wrapped itself round her. She was quite bewildered by the sudden storm, and stood still, watching it, wasting precious seconds. All at once she realized that she was in danger. She tried desperately to collect her thoughts but her mind felt heavy and muddled, and her limbs reluctant to move.

'I must run, I must run,' she kept saying to herself as she stood swaying in the coils of mist which clung round her body. Her eyes closed. She couldn't keep them open any longer. She felt terribly tired and longed just to sleep. The Rose tumbled to the ground. Gradually Melissa sank to her knees and then fell on to the grass in a deep slumber.

Mantari, who had sheltered from the rain beneath a hedge, crept out. He took the fallen Rose in his mouth and fled from the little square. As Melissa slept, the mist still rising in little puffs around her, a tall figure bent over her. It stretched down a hand, on which was a ring set with a ruby the size of a pomegranate, and picked her limp body up. Then it vanished in the air.

13

Sebastian was now extremely worried. He had walked round the maze several times and had found no sign of Melissa or Mantari. He had tried to force his way through the hedge at various points, but it had been stubborn and not yielded an inch. He had heard the crash of thunder and seen the sky grow dark overhead. He was afraid that Melissa was in great danger, and had no idea what to do next.

'It's obviously no good trying to get into the maze,' he thought to himself, 'it just isn't going to let me. I hate this beastly garden. It looks so beautiful, and it's positively nasty. Everything in it is under the Enchanter's evil. Just a minute, though? Not quite everything. That bird tried to help us, didn't it? Unless it was trying to trap us. It could have deliberately sent us into the maze so that we'd get lost or something. It does seem, though, as if I'll have to trust it. I can't think of anything else to do.'

So he set off across the pink grass in search of the bird, with the uncomfortable feeling that someone was watching every step he took. He went back to the rose bushes where the bird had sung to them, but there was no sign of it. The fountain too was deserted. The only moving things in sight were the flowers and water.

'This is ridiculous,' he thought to himself, 'that bird must have been in with the Enchanter all along.'

He sat down on the grass and put his head in his hands. He felt tired, and the dreamy feeling, which the children had noticed when they first entered the garden, crept over him again. He was trying hard to think of some way to find Melissa, but his mind kept wandering and he found himself staring very hard at the grass by his feet. It seemed to be moving around in circles and patterns, and yet each blade was quite still. Suddenly he realized that there was a voice coming from the tree behind him. It was very quiet, almost a whisper. He looked up, and there, peeping between the leaves, was the ivory bird. 'Danger', it sang over and over again in its sweet voice. Sebastian stood up and at once the bird hopped on to his shoulder.

It put its beak close to his ear and whispered, 'Come into the shelter of the trees.'

Sebastian did as he was told, and, when they were quite hidden under the feathery branches, he said, 'please could you tell me where Melissa is? It's terribly important that I find her.'

The bird put its head on one side and looked at Sebastian through its violet eye. 'The Enchanter, the Enchanter, the Enchanter,' it sang. Then it flew into the air and fluttered off over the trees. Sebastian followed it, keeping all the time in the shadow of the trees and bushes. It took him into a part of the garden he had never seen before, and the further he went the more he felt that someone was watching him. He was sure now that the Enchanter had got Melissa, and the creepy feeling he had was so strong that every time a twig caught on his clothes he jumped nervously, thinking that someone had touched him. He didn't notice the beauty of the garden any longer, every part of him was tense, and alert for danger. He began to wonder if this was all part of the Enchanter's plan and that he was being led into a trap, but then, rounding some bushes, he saw what the bird had wished to show him.

Rising up before him was a great palace which shone and glittered, its pointed towers spiking the purple sky, and it was made entirely of glass. He could see through the walls into the rooms and through those rooms into more rooms beyond. The floors were glass too. Above and below, every inch of the house was visible from wherever one stood, and there, high up at the top of one of the crystal towers sat Melissa. Her red dress shone out through the walls and she was weeping bitterly. Sebastian was dismayed. He now knew exactly where she was, but how could he get her out without being seen himself? All the other rooms looked quite empty, and there was no sign of the Enchanter, but he might come back at any moment, or, horrible thought, he might have turned himself invisible and be waiting in the castle for him. Then Sebastian shook himself. He was being silly, there was no reason for the Enchanter to know that Melissa had not come to the garden alone. All the same he couldn't just walk straight in. If he got caught as well that would probably be the end of both of them. He had to get Melissa out somehow though, so how was it to be managed? He thought back over his past adventures. He had always been helped by good magic and it was clear that he was going to need its help now. The bird was nowhere to be seen however. Apparently it had done all it could. Suddenly he remembered the Emerald in his pocket. The Teapot had been able to do some pretty fair magic and the Emerald was more powerful. It seemed his only hope. He took the Emerald from his pocket and held it in the palm of his hand. It sparkled there for a moment and then it gradually began to fade. Sebastian watched the colour die away until there was just a green glow in the centre. Then he felt himself begin to prickle all over and his body began to stiffen. And just as the last glow of colour left the Emerald and it became a mere piece of glass, the hand which held it became clear and brittle too, and quite transparent. Sebastian looked down at himself. Yes. The Emerald had turned him into glass. He took a step forward, and found that he could move quite easily, although not as well as when he was ordinary flesh and blood. It was very strange to see the grass flatten under his glass boots. When he touched his leg with his hand there was a chinking sound and he couldn't feel anything.

'I shall have to be careful not to chip myself,' he thought, and then he put the Emerald back into his stiff glassy pocket and edged his way towards the house. He was aware that although he was made of glass, his outline would still be visible among the bright colours of the garden, so he was careful to keep in the shadow of the trees. At last he reached an enormous glass door in the front of the house, and there was still no sign of life. He turned the handle as quietly as possible, and slipped inside.

A large flight of stairs was before him and he trod their smooth, slippery surface as quickly as he could without sliding off them. It was very difficult not to make a noise, and now and then a little chime rang out in the silence, when his foot struck the step too sharply. He slithered to the top, and found himself in a large room. The emerald sun and the gold moon wheeled past him, clearly visible through the brittle walls and the garden was spread out below him. All the furniture in the room was made of glass. There were shining crystal tables and carved glass chairs. Rows of cupboards and gleaming coffers, full of onyx and marble jars and smoking flasks, trembling and bubbling with spells. In the centre of the room was a glass tree, a delicate confusion of twisted branches, and from its leaves flowed drops of water like tears. They never seemed to reach the ground, for there was not a speck of water on the smooth glass floor, but as they fell, they changed from pink to blue, from green to yellow, and from purple to pink again, a never-ending rainbow fountain. For a moment

Sebastian watched it, fascinated, but not for long. He knew that delay was dangerous. He looked up through the ceiling and saw Melissa's red dress far above him. In each corner of the room was a narrow spiral staircase which wound up to each of the towers on the edge of the house. He was just setting off towards the one which led up to Melissa's room, when the Emerald tumbled out of his pocket and crashed on to the floor, where it slid with a teeth-jarring squeak until it reached the leg of a large table.

'Shh!' said Sebastian frantically, and looked round quickly hoping that no one had heard. He crept over to it and picked it up. 'How on earth did that happen?' he wondered. Then he understood. Lying on the table was a large glass key. He would never have seen it if the Emerald hadn't led him over to it. He put the Emerald back into his pocket and picked up the key. Then he began to climb the spiral staircase, twisting and turning until he felt quite dizzy, and all the time watching out for the return of the Enchanter. At last he reached the top of the staircase and could see Melissa quite clearly through the walls of her room. He fitted the key into the glass lock and it turned easily. Melissa looked up to see the door opening slowly and something clear and shiny coming into the room. She was terribly frightened, and opened her mouth to cry out. Just in time she saw it put a glassy finger to its lips, and heard it say, 'Shh, it's me! Don't make a noise for heaven's sake!' so the scream came out as a little squeak.

When she realized who it was, she could have cried with relief, but fortunately she was a sensible girl and decided that crying could wait till later.

'Sebastian!' she whispered, 'I thought I'd never see you again. I'm sorry I was stupid enough to get caught.'

'Never mind that now,' said Sebastian, 'the thing is to get out of here. Do you know where the Enchanter is.'

'He's gone to look for the Rose. I found it and picked it,

and then the rain sent me to sleep and I must have dropped it. I woke up here and the Enchanter was absolutely furious that I didn't have it.'

'Right,' said Sebastian, thinking quickly. 'We'll have to forget about the Rose for the moment, and concentrate on getting out of here while he's in the garden. Let's hope the Emerald can make you glass, too.'

He took the Emerald out of his pocket and handed it to her. Just as she took it in her hand, there was a tremendous crash below them, and Melissa said 'ouch' very loudly. Sebastian looked down through the floor and saw, to his dismay, that the crash had been made by the front door slamming shut. A tall, thin man, with a face the colour of alabaster, was in the room below them. He was pacing up and down, clenching his fists and fuming with anger.

'Oh, heavens,' he said, turning to Melissa. 'We're stuck now...' And then he broke off in astonishment for Melissa was standing clutching her finger, looking very pale, and blood was simply pouring on to the white rug at her feet.

'I cut myself on the Emerald,' she said shakily. 'It doesn't actually hurt, but I've never seen so much blood before.'

And indeed the rug was now a bright crimson all over, just the colour of Melissa's dress.

'I see what's happened,' whispered Sebastian, 'the Emerald did it on purpose. When the Enchanter looks up, he'll see the rug covered with blood and he'll think it's you. Meanwhile we can be making our escape.'

'Of course!' said Melissa, 'that really was very clever of it. My finger's stopped bleeding now. Let's hurry.'

She held the colourless Emerald firmly in her hand, and turned the glass right under Sebastian's eyes. He was so fascinated watching this, that he almost forgot they were in a hurry, but Melissa took him by the hand and pulled him through the door to the top of the spiral staircase.

134

They were just trying to decide, in whispers, how they were going to get past the Enchanter, when an awful thing happened. Somebody, neither was sure who it was, slipped on the smooth surface at the head of the stairs and they grabbed at each other in a frantic attempt to save themselves tumbling headlong to the bottom. There was a loud jangle of glass and then they managed to get their balance again, but not before the key had fallen from Sebastian's hand and gone chinking and bouncing all the way down the stairs. It shattered in tiny pieces at the Enchanter's feet. The Enchanter stopped his pacing and bent down to pick up the glass fragments. He examined them closely and then looked up to the tower where Melissa had been imprisoned. For an awful moment the children thought that he must be able to see them, but he just looked away and over to the table on which the key should have been. At this point the children waited no longer. They ran as fast as they possibly could along the corridor leading from Melissa's room to the tower on the other corner of the house. There they found a spiral staircase leading down to the large room. Sebastian saw that the Enchanter had started to climb the stair to Melissa's tower.

'Run!' he said to the glass shape beside him, and they flew down the stairs as fast as their stiff limbs allowed them, across the large hall and down the main stairs to the front door. Just as they got there, they heard a roar of anger and they knew that the Enchanter had discovered the trick.

'Come on,' shouted Sebastian. He wrenched open the front door and pulled Melissa through. The door slammed behind them. He turned and saw the Enchanter thundering down the staircase at tremendous speed. The children set off across the garden, willing their glass legs to move more quickly and expecting any minute to feel an icy hand grip the backs of their necks.

'To the tunnel,' yelled Sebastian, 'and don't look back!'

'Where's Mantari?' gasped Melissa suddenly. 'I haven't seen him since the rain sent me to sleep. Supposing the Enchanter's got him! We can't leave him here.'

'We'll have to,' said Sebastian, 'he'll find his own way back. Just keep running.'

Melissa felt terrible about leaving Mantari to the mercy of the Enchanter, but Sebastian took hold of her hand and refused to let her slow down. Presently it became much easier to run and they found that they had turned back into ordinary human beings. The Emerald burned bright and green in Sebastian's hand and its brilliance seemed to give them a new strength. Also they could hear someone crashing through the trees behind them, which spurred them on to run faster than either of them had ever run in their lives before. As they passed the fountain several birds rose from the bushes and swept over the children's heads, soaring and circling, with loud cries. They went out of sight and suddenly the children heard a rapid beating of wings and howls of rage and pain. The children were too exhausted with the effort of running to speak, but they both grinned inside themselves, for they knew that the birds were attacking the Enchanter and holding him back. Just as the end of the tunnel came in sight, Melissa saw out of the corner of her eye that something was running beside her. She looked round quickly. It was Mantari. He was leaping along, his yellow eyes beaming, and the green rose clenched between his teeth. She was just about to shout to Sebastian to tell him that Mantari was with them, when she saw there was no need. He had already seen him, and he flashed a grin at Melissa to show that he was every bit as pleased and relieved as she was.

As they came up to the mouth of the tunnel, the cries of the birds came closer and there was a thudding of feet on the grass just behind them and a great shout of fury. Mantari and the children shot into the tunnel. Then there was the sound of rocks crashing down, and they found themselves in darkness. As soon as Sebastian could catch his breath he gave a cry of relief. 'Look! The entrance to the tunnel's blocked. We're saved!'

14

The Emerald throbbed in the darkness. It had quite
worn itself out, in its efforts to thwart the Enchanter. As
soon as their hearts had stopped thumping unbearably,
they all set off as fast as they could up the steps of the
tunnel, for they knew that the Enchanter would find
another way to get to the Treasure House and they didn't
have a moment to lose. Their only comfort was that now
that they had the Rose, the Enchanter wouldn't be
able to use magic, so they had at least a chance to get there
before him.

Guided by the light of Mantari's eyes, they scrambled up
the endless flight, legs aching and lungs bursting. At last
they reached the top and were running along the sloping
passage. Each of them secretly felt that they couldn't keep
it up much longer, but forced themselves onwards for the
sake of the others. At last they burst out of the tunnel into
fresh air. The horses were standing by the entrance, stamping the ground, and impatient to be off. It was such a relief
to see them, and to have ordinary blue sky over their heads
and green grass under their feet, that they all found just
enough energy to clamber on to the broad white backs and
bury their hands into the glossy manes. Mantari crouched
in front of Melissa, the Rose still firmly between his teeth,
and they were off.

The speed at which they swept over the ground made

the previous ride seem like a gentle canter. The horses bunched their powerful muscles and flew. They jumped right over trees and hills and anything which stood in their way. The sky grew dark and angry, and yellow flashes like spear shafts drove themselves into the ground, shattering the valleys with blinding light. Peals of thunder tore the sky and the wind howled and raged above them.

Behind them rode the Enchanter, in a great chariot of flames which streamed out their burning light against the sky and smouldered around his white face, in which his eyes glittered, more deadly than the fiercest fire. His chariot was pulled by six straining black beasts. Their hooves pounded the earth and their nostrils steamed as they devoured the ground before them. At last the children rose into the air and soared over the great wall which surrounded the Enchanter's Treasure House.

The stream stood up on end and lashed its water against them. The trees howled and stretched out their stringy hands to grab them, tearing at their very roots in the effort to snatch the children from their horses. Scratched and torn they reached the great door and half jumped, half fell on to the steps. The door swung wide and the candles leapt and smouldered as the wind rushed through the House. Sebastian, Melissa and Mantari raced along the corridors to the gold and silver room. Melissa grabbed the Teapot from the table where they had left it, and Sebastian wrenched the Mirror from the wall.

'The Well!' he shouted, 'where is it?'

Horror dawned on Melissa's face. They had forgotten to find out exactly where it was before setting out. Mantari gave a great howl and ran to the door. Without a word the children pelted down the stairs after him. He ran along the corridor, past the Room of Books and into a part of the House which Sebastian had never seen before. They came to a flight of worn stone steps and Mantari flew down them without hesitating.

'The dungeons. Of course!' panted Melissa, and at that moment a roar shook the House. All the candles guttered and then went out, and they knew the Enchanter had arrived. Down the steps they fled, sometimes missing one and landing on the next with a jarring bump. Mantari was waiting for them at the bottom. As soon as he saw them he stood up on his hind legs for a moment, and then dashed off into the darkness. They followed him along a stone passage, barred windows and heavy iron doors glinting on either side, and horrible, spiky, metal machines looming up in the shadows. The children weren't sure what they were for, but both made their private guesses and felt a chill of horror. Their footsteps rang on the stone floors and the damp walls threw back the echo of their gasps. At last they came into a large room, bare but for a round, low wall in the centre. A green light shone up from inside it and cast a wavering, leaping glow over the rough brickwork. They heard the sound of water bubbling, which was rapidly drowned by the noise of heavy footsteps coming along the corridor towards them.

'Come on,' shouted Sebastian, 'not a second to lose!' and he threw the Mirror, the Rose and the Teapot into the foaming depths of the Well and pushed Melissa in after them. A jet of green water spurted up and splashed the walls, and she sank from sight at once. Just as Sebastian grabbed Mantari and put his leg over to jump in, something gripped his arm. The cold white fingers of the Enchanter dug deep into his flesh and he saw the glittering black eyes only a few inches from his own. The teeth were bared in a grin of triumph.

Mantari hissed and sprang. He ripped his claws through the white skin and black blood oozed into the wounds. The Enchanter gave a scream of pain and loosened his hold on

Sebastian's arm just for a second. That second was enough though. Wrenching himself free Sebastian seized Mantari and leapt into the well. As he sank, he saw the Enchanter's face above him, staring down. Then it began to spin. Round and round it went. The eyes grew huge and the mouth gaped open. Then the water bubbled over and Sebastian could see no more. He could feel himself sinking down and down, a rush of foaming water in his ears. It was difficult to see anything for the water churned about him and whirled him round, tossed him upside down and flung him up again. Bubbles rushed up from his nose and mouth and he longed to draw breath. Then he felt the violence of the water grow less and his mind began to drift and grow drowsy. He wondered if he were drowning, for he had heard that it was like going to sleep after the first dreadful panic. He felt peaceful and the water lapped soothingly against him.

Suddenly there was a deafening crash and something hit him hard on the arm. He opened his eyes and sat up. He was sitting on the floorboards of the attic. The chair which he had used to get up to the Mirror was lying on its side and the Teapot had rolled into a corner. Sebastian got up and rubbed his bruised elbow tenderly. He was quite dry. There was not a drop of water or a speck of mud to be seen. His clothes were neat and tidy, and his hair was no more disorderly than it usually was.

He went over to the Mirror and took a close look at it. The dull, green glass was still, there was no sign of life. It seemed almost like an ordinary, tarnished looking-glass. He picked up the Teapot, dragged the chair back into the corner, and went slowly down to the kitchen. Just as he had put the Teapot back on its shelf, he heard the front door open, and several pairs of feet clattered down the stairs.

'Hallo, dear,' said Mrs Parkin as she came into the kitchen. 'What have you been up to while we've been out? My, you should have seen some of the people there today...' and she bustled about, unpinning her hat and putting the kettle on and talking all at once. Then the others came in and they all sat down to tea.

The next day the house was a frenzy of activity. Everyone was busy getting ready for the arrival of the Master and the new Mistress. Sheets were aired, furniture was polished, and everything was scrubbed to a shining cleanliness.

Sebastian felt rather in the way. He kept offering to help but they all seemed to manage better on their own. He wandered around restlessly, one half of him thrilled and happy at the thought of seeing his father again, and the other half worried and anxious about Melissa. It was possible that the magic might have gone wrong. She might be worse off now than before, and the terrible thing was that he would never know.

As he was sitting in the library, flicking through some books and quite unable to concentrate, Sarah came in.

'There you are,' she said, 'I've got a job for you. I found this old looking-glass in the attic and Mrs Parkin says to hang it over the fireplace. I've given it a clean and it's come up lovely. Shouldn't be surprised if it isn't quite valuable—real silver, you know. Can't think why it's been shut up there all that time. Bring over that chair will you, love?'

Sebastian brought the chair over and held the Mirror against the wall while Sarah got the hammer and nails. His own face looked back at him from its clean, gleaming surface. Not a thread of smoke remained to show that it had once been a far from ordinary looking-glass.

'That's that bit of magic over, then,' he thought to himself, as he stepped back to admire it with Sarah.

In bed that night he lay awake staring at the ceiling long after the rest of the house had gone to sleep, reliving all the adventures of the past few weeks and always returning to the inevitable question—what had happened to Melissa? At last he fell asleep from sheer exhaustion. He dreamed that he was standing before the gates of the Treasure House once more. But this time they were wide open. He walked up the long twisting drive until he came to the bend which brought the House in full view. There he stopped with a gasp of astonishment. The once beautiful, towering mansion was in ruins. The front door stood open, sagging on its hinges. The delicate stonework was crumbled and broken. He walked through the doorway into the corridor he remembered as a long tunnel, ablaze with candles. Now only the walls remained. Fingers of daylight searched out its darkest recesses. Here and there a few candles in their holders jutted out into the clear smokeless air, their wax hardened into crusty knobs. In his dream, as he surveyed the piles of dust and shattered stonework that lay before him, he heard someone call his name.

'Sebastian, Sebastian. Over here!'

He began to run towards the voice, along the winding corridors and up the stairs which led to her room. But, alas, only five or six of those broad sweeping steps remained, overgrown with a mass of white sweet-scented flowers and where the little oak door had been, there was a huge expanse of sky.

He ran back through the corridors and out into the garden.

'Melissa!' he shouted, 'where are you?'

Then he saw her. She was standing in the shadow of some trees, her dress glowing a deeper crimson than ever and her soft hair blowing around her face as if a gentle breeze were hovering over her.

'Melissa!' said Sebastian, 'wait there. Don't go away,' and he began to walk quickly towards her. But he couldn't seem to get any closer. He kept walking and walking but the distance between them never got smaller.

'I don't understand,' he said. 'Does it mean that we're never to be together again?'

He stopped, and in spite of himself he felt a lump come into his throat. 'Is that what it means?' he asked again.

She spoke, and her voice seemed to come from somewhere beside him. 'We are from a different time, Sebastian. Don't be unhappy. My guardian has awoken from a terrible dream while he slept by the fire and will never be troubled by nightmares again. I have everything I want, and it is only in my dreams that I visit this place again. My imprisonment is over and the magic is almost finished.'

'Almost?' said Sebastian. His heart felt heavy and there were tears pricking his eyelids. He had never realized, in the short time he had known her, how much she had come to mean to him.

'Sebastian,' she said, and there was great happiness in her voice, 'very soon, I promise you, you will understand and the magic will be finished.'

'But Melissa,' cried Sebastian, 'we could have...we could have,' but he couldn't say any more. He knew in his heart of hearts that they had only been a tiny part of the magic and that whatever they wanted to happen, it had all been settled a hundred years ago.

'Goodbye,' he said softly, 'I'm glad you're happy. It was what we wanted after all, wasn't it?'

Melissa said nothing, but in the shadows he could see something glinting on her cheeks.

He started to run towards her, he was shouting something, he didn't know what, but the crimson faded and she was gone.

As Sebastian awoke, with a terrible pain in his heart, he felt a tear fall on his face, and he heard her voice for the last time.

'Not quite finished,' she whispered, 'not yet, not yet.'

15

The morning came, bright and cold. After breakfast Sebastian went up to the library, for there were to be no lessons that day because of the Master's arrival, and Sebastian didn't want to go for a walk in case his father came while he was out. So instead he started a new painting and all the time he turned over the dream in his mind, puzzling over the words he had heard as he awoke, and wondering what they could mean. The painting was of Mantari. He drew him very large, and tried to make each whisker stand out separately, to give his coat the sheen he remembered, and bring the bright orange colour to life. It was very difficult, and he was thoroughly absorbed in it when there was the sound of a carriage drawing up outside.

Flinging down his paintbrush, Sebastian rushed to the window. Yes, there was his father climbing out of the carriage—and there were two people with him. One was a tall, graceful woman who he knew at once must be his step-mother. The other was a young girl. He couldn't see her face for it was hidden by a large-brimmed bonnet. How strange! Could this be the surprise his father had mentioned in his letters? But he didn't wait any longer to see.

In no time at all he was downstairs and in his father's arms.

'Papa!' he cried. 'I'm so glad you're home.'

His father was so pleased to see him that for a moment he couldn't say anything. But after the first wonderful excitement was over, he turned to the woman who stood beside him and said, in a voice full of fatherly pride, 'Mary, this is my son. Sebastian, this is my wife whom I want you to love as much as I do.'

Sebastian looked at the woman who was now to be a part of his life, and took the hand she held out to him.

'I hope we'll be very good friends indeed, Sebastian,' she said, and her voice was gentle and full of kindness. And, as he looked at her smiling face and warm brown eyes, somehow he knew that they would be.

Suddenly she bent down and kissed him and he found that he didn't mind at all. It seemed perfectly natural in fact, for an immediate bond of affection had sprung up between them.

Then his step-mother put her arm through his, and led him over to the person who stood waiting in the shadows.

'And now for the surprise your father wrote to you about,' she said. 'I want you to meet my daughter, Selina. Her father died when she was about the same age as you were when you lost your mother, so up till now she has led a fairly lonely life and she and I have been everything to each other. Now all that has changed and we are a complete family again. Your father thought that you would like to have a young person in the house and it was his idea to keep it as a surprise. You are about the same age, and it would make me very happy if you were good friends.'

The girl, Selina, stepped into the light and held out a neatly gloved hand towards Sebastian. He took it...and then his heart missed a beat. From under the fashionable bonnet, the green eyes looked at him steadily, and she smiled.

147

'How do you do,' she said, in a voice that was as familiar to Sebastian as his own. But there was no tone of recognition in her voice and her eyes seemed to see him for the first time. Sebastian could think of nothing to say, he just stood in silence, and looked, and wondered.

How could it be that she looked so like...? Those eyes... and the whiteness of her skin! The mouth in a wide smile just as he remembered it. The fine, elegant clothes made a difference, of course, and it was difficult to see clearly in the dimness of the hall lamps, but still the likeness was incredible! Could it be...could it possibly be...?

The girl stood waiting for him to reply, and seemed slightly puzzled by his silence.

Sebastian slowly felt his heart sink, and the bitterest disappointment seized him. How foolish of him. How foolish to have let his imagination send his hopes soaring skywards only to be dashed so completely. How could he have believed for an instant, that his wildest dream had been fulfilled. Anguish filled him, and he could only just restrain himself from giving way.

Then he became aware that the others were looking at him, wondering why he didn't speak.

'I'm so pleased you have come to live here,' he forced himself to murmur.

There was an almost audible sigh of relief from those around him. Then his father led the way up to the library and William came to take the luggage in, and in the general activity the awkward moment was forgotten.

Sebastian was very angry with himself though, for nearly spoiling his father's home-coming, so he put himself out to tell them all his news and to listen attentively to what was being said. And it wasn't very difficult for his step-mother was an intelligent person and talked very amusingly, and Selina was really very charming and natural. His father sat and listened most of the time but

148

Sebastian could tell that he felt very contented and happy to be home. From time to time his eyes would rest fondly on Sebastian and then he would glance over to his wife and smile. It seemed that he was very glad to have a proper family again. And Sebastian noticed that this warmth of feeling extended towards Selina as well, and that although she called him 'sir' it was said with a great deal of love and affection. Sebastian knew that it was up to him to forget about his feelings of disappointment, and make the circle complete.

At last Mrs Parkin came up to announce that lunch was ready, so the grown-ups went to change after their long journey, and his father suggested that the two children should join them downstairs in a few minutes.

As soon as they were left alone, Selina took off her bonnet and shook the pretty brown ringlets that framed her face.

'Phew! that's better,' she said, 'these wretched things are so hot.' She smiled at him and Sebastian smiled back as warmly as he could. He was beginning to like her in her own right, and he was determined to make up for his former ungraciousness.

Selina got up and went over to the table where all his painting things were spread out.

'I say, did you do this,' she said, glancing down at the sheet of paper which was still wet. 'It's awfully good. Have you any more? I really would like to see them. Please may I?'

Sebastian felt slightly embarrassed about showing his work to strangers, but he knew it was something he would have to get over, and anyway, he wasn't in a position to refuse her anything.

As he got up to show them to her, Selina picked up the pencil which lay among the paintbrushes and quickly scribbled something. Sebastian leaned over her shoulder to see what she had written. Then his heart almost stopped beating. He turned to the girl beside him, and her face was lit by a strange radiance, and her green eyes shone as she smiled and smiled. Then he put out his hand towards her and a joy and happiness flowed between, so great that it could never be put into words.

Below his paintings of the orange cat, in large hasty letters, was the one word 'MANTARI'.